The Adventure
Penelope Toomey
and other stories

by

Christine Collette

Circaidy Gregory Press

Copyright information

This collection under this cover © 2011, Kay Green. The copyright to all works, including images contained in the text © 2011, Christine Frances Collette. 'Weather Report' first published as 'Weather Report from France', Countryside Tales Summer 2010 issue 42. 'The Dream' and 'The Market' first published, The Writers' Group, Civray, 2011. 'Tom Christmas' first published, 'recognition' Earlyworks Press, 2009 Cover design © Kay Green 2011. Cover photo © Christine Frances Collette 1994

All rights reserved. No part of this publication may be reproduced, stored in a retrieval system, rebound or transmitted in any form or for any purpose without the prior written permission of the publisher. This book is sold subject to the condition that it shall not be lent, resold, hired out or otherwise circulated without the publisher's prior consent in any form or binding other than that in which it is published.

paperback ISBN 978-1-906451-52-3
ebook ISBN 978-1-906451-47-9

Printed in the UK
By MPG Books Group

Published by Circaidy Gregory Press
Creative Media Centre
45 Robertson St, Hastings
Sussex TN34 1HL

www.circaidygregory.co.uk

Dedication

à l'équipe

Contents

The adventures of Penelope Toomey
    Pigs' Delight   1
    Bandsman   5
    Boulogne   13
    Paris   24
    Amsterdam   29
    Roger's Wedding   38

Tom Christmas   41

Loves and Lives
    Circumstances   61
    The Sylph and the Stag   62
    The Brown Cardigan   65
    The Moustache   66
    The Cigarette   70
    The Dream   74
    Whoopsie   77
    Weather Report   79

The Village
    Ch–1   83
    The Wild Boar Hunt   85
    The Market   86
    Life in France   89
    We Walk   91

Louise Maigret and her Jules   92

Lady Audley's Revenge   102

Epilogue
    The Election of God   115

Pigs' Delight

This is a middle-of-the-night book for tubby women who get hot flushes, wrote Pigs (Penelope) Toomey.

Pigs liked wine, hand-rolling tobacco, and she had her list of discs ready should she ever be called to *Desert Island*. She was awake now, contemplating with much awe her mountain of debts. *These are the hopes of a hopeful person,* wrote Pigs. She was a round, brown person with a round face decorated with round glasses and brown, corkscrew hair. She had a surprised expression from the permanent frown that swung up into the corkscrews. Arms and legs were also round, knees round on her legs like the spectacles on the face. It was wondrous, thought Pigs, how one aged overnight as body fat redistributed itself around the menopausal frame, collecting in what Anita Brookner called 'untidiness' about the hips. The face, once surprised by the first laughter-line wrinkles, now collected itself in slack pouches under the jaw.

Pigs' mother, seeking to fulfil the self-imposed role of matriarch to an extended family, had once hired a hit man, to teach a (less than final) lesson to a brutal male in-law. The offender had been reprieved at the eleventh hour by his patronne's cold feet. Belated mercy had also been shown the many people represented by the wax effigies Pigs' mother had made, attacked, buried and then dug up. Such vacillation was not a common feature of Pigs' family, who tended rather to the individual or collective rush, both feet forward, and never look back. Pigs had often to remind herself that just because one Knew Best, it did not mean one was right. Indeed, a further cause of awe was the realisation that, very often, having been totally in the right in a given situation, Recording Angels surely remarking her selflessness, patience, perspicacity, longsuffering and general moral rectitude, Pigs was revealed, with hindsight, to be woefully wrong.

The thing about a middle-of-the-night book, Pigs decided, was that it should be neither too deep nor too shallow; it should not deprive a sweating, anxious female of sleep but rather divert her from the terrors of daily existence. Pigs believed firmly that one should follow one's dream, climb one's mountains, with Julie Andrews' voice but not her face, scale the heights, jump guns and set sights – and she preferred books that told her so. Characters in debt were always welcome. Their situations should contain as much comfort (ease, rather than elegance, or riches) as possible; lit grates, cosy chats, steamy tearooms, inns, garden benches met these requirements. Pigs called these tea-and-toast, old-clothes books and quite often found them masquerading as detective stories, Raymond Chandler included. A good-looking hero had once been an attraction but he had given way to a preference for jolly characters, dauntless, witty women and cheerful men. Biographies were pretty good, except for the almost invariable parting with the subject on her or his deathbed; a lowering, not at all middle-of-the-night procedure. Should Pigs write a biography, she would start with the death to get it over so that she could end in the prime of her subject's life. Pigs, however, preferred to write a novel. It will be seen that she was rather fond of Stevie Smith; she would fill her night with words that her night might gleam; blind her sight with visions that her horrors might fade.

On the sands at S—t there are ridges left by the tide of water one seldom sees. The sand is reality, the sea is imagined depth, encompassing the horizon of one's vision. There are clues and hints of the depth: smelt, felt by the thrusting feet. Once Pigs saw many dead birds. There is a nineteen-fifties pier, bare boards with big gaps that frighten the children and, far at the end, huts where plastic cups of tea are sold in a steamy tearoom. There is a train carrying people to Desolation. Inland, there is a different train with a Thomas Tank face in which Pigs once spied a boy delighted, riding, riding.

Pigs' mother sang songs when she could not sleep. Pigs had not seriously tried this, but she sometimes arranged the Desert Discs. The first one started:

There's a little white duck
Floating on the water
A little white duck
Doing as he oughta

...and it would be nice to know what came next, hidden from Pigs' consciousness for about thirty years. This song vied for first preference with: *She wears red feathers and a hula-hula skirt* which used to be sung by Pigs and her friend Patty, either end of a long, dark corridor down which they dashed madly to and fro.

Runaway (Del Shannon – keep up!) came next and had introduced Boys. Boys were, collectively, a phenomenon. To help deal with them Pigs wore, at various times, pan-stick make up, green face powder, and American Tan seamless stockings. The stockings had holes around the knees, and the point of not wearing seams was that one could reverse front to back to hide the holes. The young Pigs frequented a café called Charlie Brown's. Charlie Brown's had linoleum on the floor and Con-tact cloth peeling off wooden tables. Dusty Springfield sang, and Elvis and Adam Faith. The best-looking Boys were undoubtedly the ones in charge of the dodgems and swing boats at the fairs (every bank holiday, so there was usually a plentiful supply of Boys present, just coming or just gone). These good-lookers were dangerously near the limits of the concept of 'Boy', edging towards something More. True Boys never liked kissing for very long, especially if the film was good, and never wanted to 'be alone'. Boys were for summer and disappeared in winter evenings when homework took over their time. Sometimes there would be a circus as well as a fair and one could look at the animal cages; a pre-Boys Pigs once spent hours screwing up her eyes in simulated feline expression which the mangy lions eventually returned; but the cage was small and smelly and sad. Also there was cricket on the same green, much beloved of Pigs' father, he who sang of little white ducks; a diffident man, but possessed of a great ability to float and wander, he had once invited himself to tea with the –shire team to reward his own persistence on the sidelines. Pigs' father was extremely wary of Boys, as of something that would eventually hurt; in which he was quite right.

One of the problems with writing a book, remembered Pigs, was that someone had already produced one's masterpiece. She had intended Ann Veronica for a number of years before finding H.G. Wells had written it for her. When Pigs was at primary school the class had been set as essay to begin: *once upon a time*. One boy, really, truthfully, had written a story: *once a pon...* which contained many delightful adventures. The old, pink, male teacher, who had a disturbing habit of crying as he chastised the boys under their short trousers, failed to meet this challenge to his imagination.

Once upon a time, wrote Pigs, *in South London in the nineteen fifties, there was a Park with swings and playing fields and a scented Garden for the Blind and, of course, a tea-room.* She firmly suppressed two paragraphs plagiarised from Virginia Woolf.

In the Park was a Bandstand; now she was cheating Elizabeth Bowen. Pigs' mother and aunt were fond of the teashop. The young Pigs crashed around the park, never confined by tea or garden. One Sunday afternoon, she left the park at the tail of a band and its following, and found herself in strange streets and Traffic. She remembered the trauma of her losing and finding. She decided to go to her present park to write, thereby escaping Woolf, Bowen, Wells, Smith, Chandler et al by rediscovering her roots. Instead of a teashop there was a bar for white wine or espresso coffee and a polished floor, as unlike Charlie Brown's as thirty years, Mary Quant and the Rolling Stones could make possible.

Pigs chewed her sugar and sucked her Espresso. The trick with Espresso was to drink it just on the cusp of too hot and lukewarm; erring on one side led to scalding, on the other to dealing with a nasty mouthful of tin. A band played. Pigs sat. They played on. She ordered, chewed, sucked. The band started to leave.

Now, thought Pigs, *I follow*. Discreetly, and to the great surprise of the last musician to pack his music case in his car boot, Pigs drove her old Peugeot in Chandler-esque pursuit. A brief circuit of suburban streets led to the motorway approach. Pigs stopped for petrol. She drove slowly, carefully, respecting the aged gears. After a forty-minute crawl she passed the next service station entrance and exit. At the exit, the Bandsman's car pulled neatly in front of her Peugeot.

I don't know if I'm on the Pier train or Thomas, thought Pon-Pigs, *but I shall write my adventures.*

The adventures of Pigs

The Bandsman

The Bandsman's car was a Mercedes, common in the area, grey metallic. Seeming to sympathise with Pigs' Peugeot, it kept to a steady sixty miles per hour and the inside lane. The next exit was an

'A' road through a particularly attractive piece of countryside, one of Pigs' favourites. The Mercedes took the exit and carried on to a big pub, a roadhouse near a canal. The Mercedes parked. Pigs, fiercely Marlowe, found a lay-by near the steps to the canal, where she rolled a Gauloise in liquorice paper. Two roll ups (skinny ones; race-horses) later, the Mercedes overtook her. Pigs followed. The process was repeated, the Mercedes stopping at a Little Chef and then another pub, Pigs laying-by. Marlowe would have had bourbon. Pigs continued with racehorses. They re-entered the town and threaded their way back to the bandstand suburbs. Parked, Pigs was proud of herself, until the Bandsman knocked on her window and invited her in for drinks. 'Your persistence merits reward,' he said.

The Bandsman's house was tall and spare, like himself. The wooden floors were polished, the rugs good and the curtains heavy. There were, unsurprisingly, a piano and shelves of recordings; the shabby armchairs could have been Pigs' own. She accepted whisky, reflecting that she was near enough home to walk, or to call her son out to meet her.

'I live alone,' said the Bandsman. 'There is no-one to disturb us.' Pigs tried to look as homely, brown and round as possible, not a difficult task. 'It is dinnertime,' he continued, 'and I should like to try a new recipe.' Perhaps he was inspired by Pigs' obvious promise of gluttony. 'Would you care to be a guinea-pig?' Forcibly struck by the coincidence of the identity he offered her, Pigs accepted. The Bandsman set music playing, generously refilled her whisky glass and disappeared. Pigs had uttered three words: 'whisky, please' and 'yes.' She marvelled at herself. She was hungry. She was comforted that she looked a little more chic in evening light, when the bones of jaw and hip seemed to reassert their prominence; on the other hand, the chances of a really bad hot flush were increased, red cheeks, short breath. She produced a notebook and began, like the Angels, to record.

At dinner there was wine. Pigs became very boring on the subject of her family. The Bandsman talked of cookery. Pigs decided to sparkle. She sparkled on a number of subjects, including food. The Bandsman, following her lead, majored on music. Neither of them mentioned cars or journeys, as an indiscretion forbidden by good manners and fine taste. Eventually, Pigs mentioned telephoning her son and the Bandsman acquiesced. Pigs' son, as was his virtue, was neither surprised nor judgmental and arrived swiftly. Pigs and the Bandsman arranged to meet the next week to attend a Proms concert for which the Bandsman had, *per cause*, tickets. Pigs had no intention of keeping the appointment.

Pigs was silent and absorbed on the short drive home. She roused herself to drink the cup of tea her son made and they sat companionably. Pigs' son, Roger, had her corkscrews, but black, worn long and tied at the nape of the neck. Roger smoked dope and Pigs breathed in the atmosphere gratefully. She did not tell him about the Bandsman. Roger mentioned his likely absence, on a trip to Hamburg for his security firm, the next weekend. They went to bed, their rooms characterised by a similar austerity, each carrying an indispensable glass of water; *A hundred years ago it would have been candles,* Pigs thought. There was something pleasant about carrying an object from the heart of the home into the spartan room.

Three hours later, Pigs was roused to a stomping, snorting noise. She sat up and pulled the duvet to her chin. She watched in horror as the door was flung open. In the glow of the light from the landing she saw a large figure and felt her corkscrews itch as the hairs on her neck rose. 'Mrs Toomey?' enquired the figure. Pigs continued to stare. '–shire Police,' he said. Pigs succeeded, by trying very hard, in not wetting the bed. More stomping and snorting was followed by an increase in Cerebi. Roger ambled after them. 'Don't worry, Mum,' he said. Pigs made frantic *come here, keep quiet,* gestures. Roger came and sat next to her. There was much shouting about the house while Pigs and her son sat silently, holding hands. The roach from the kitchen was carried into the room in triumph. Pigs and her son were arrested for Possession. They were allowed to dress and Pigs was allowed to visit the lavatory, albeit in police company. At the station she was sure that, briefly, at a distance, she saw the Bandsman.

The questioning lasted for several hours. Pigs was most conscious of boredom. They were questioned together and separately; she was sure Roger would be able to take care of himself. Yes, she replied, they occasionally smoked; she never bought; she did not ask her son from where he obtained supplies. These answers had been agreed between them years before and sometimes, after newsworthy local raids, rehearsed; they were also true. No, she was not morally offended by cannabis; yes, she was offended by the drug trade; no, they never supplied third parties; yes, she saw the wisdom of desisting. They left the police station together, charges having been dropped on their collective and several promises of good behaviour and stopped at a coffee stall. Roger approached a man he knew and returned with a joint, of which he offered a puff. Pigs puffed briefly. She thought hard about the evanescent Bandsman. *I did not sparkle,* she thought. *I was silly. I gave him all the evidence for this.*

Pigs was the worse for wear at work the next day. This did not matter, because the men with whom she worked were rarely in mint condition and, after lunch, fell into one of two categories; somnolent, or brash and aggressive. Pigs rather liked her job, however. She was selling advertising space, having been made redundant from her local authority housing office. Now an enabler, rather than a provider in the housing market, the local authority had celebrated its new role by office eviction on a grand scale. Pigs did not, therefore, suffer from feeling she had been singled out for poor treatment but benefited by the diminution of her responsibilities. The space-selling job was too trifling to take seriously, she was self-employed and, theoretically, could work what hours she chose, although prolonged absences during the selling day were frowned on. There was some sexual harassment from the clients, but this did not commonly survive a face-to-face interview. Her colleagues, when not post-prandially depressed, were cheerful, being burdened neither with dilemmas of principle nor requirements to engage in demanding and selfless tasks. Pigs had once spent a happy afternoon drawing a chair to advertise a local furniture shop. She liked the print process, the precision of the type and the colouring. Now and again she wrote some editorial copy and despite her tendency to edge in a small campaign on behalf of a favourite cause, the copy was nearly always accepted. And she could use the computer, of course, á la Stevie Smith, to write her own stuff.

Now, Pigs was busy copying up her notes on the weekend. It occurred to her that she did not know what instrument the Bandsman played in performance. He had talked of his violin but she had not seen what went into the music case lodged in the Mercedes' boot. It was, Pigs supposed, violin-sized overall, but she could not remember if it was violin-shaped. Music cases were notorious in fiction; they hid guns in James Bond, drugs reasonably often. Had the Bandsman picked up the music case each time he left his parked car? She did not know, having kept her careful distance.

Pigs decided to space sell to musical instrument makers. An unusual line, it proved reasonably successful. The free sheet for which she sold went to schools, pubs and clubs, which might be interested. A nice little bit of copy on summer bands in parks would be a good accompaniment and the local authority entertainment officer should prove useful. There were spin-offs into pub music nights, sheet music and record stores. Pigs went to her editor and first sold him the idea of a special feature and got permission to reduce rates for full and half colour pages. She settled down to sell in earnest, diving to and fro among her lists of possibilities. Since *Yellow Pages* were now less readily available, fewer people advertised there and cross-referencing was not so easy; but *Melody Maker* and *Exchange & Mart* helped. By the end of the afternoon Pigs had sales enough to consider propitiating the God of the Debt Mountain; but He was apt to be sniffy about small oblations so she decided on a take-away curry instead. She felt her son needed some motherly interest.

Roger had just got into the tea-and-dressing-gown stage when she arrived home. He blanched, rather, at the curry, so Pigs stored it in the cold oven and joined in the toast stakes, which she won by a short head. 'Will you be alright tonight, Mum?' asked Roger. Alarmed at this unusual proceeding, Pigs waved buttery fingers at him. 'Its just the police...' he explained. Soothed, and gratified by the attention, Pigs told him she would be fine, she'd got the curry. He went to bathe. Pigs flopped into the conservatory, warm with evening sun and turned on the radio. Idly, she snipped deadheads from a sizeable collection of half-hardy plants. She would eat out here, she decided, thinking of the hot house in *The Big Sleep* and wondering if Marlow-esque inspiration would ensue. Description of Irish characters in American novels would make a good study, she thought, the Stateside view of Republicanism mediated through fiction.

Pigs was nearly late for *The Archers* and, had she not hurried to switch channels, would have missed the significance of the broadcast from which she changed. It was the last item that had been played in the Sunday band programme, now given by the Royal Philharmonic. Pigs wrote the details on the back of a seed packet. She would ask the Bandsman about it. No, she caught herself up; she was not going to see the Bandsman again. She joined *The Archers* halfway through; she had always rather fancied being Elizabeth. Shula was too Julie Andrews. It was a short bolt from *The Archers* to *Coronation Street* on the black and white television set in the kitchen. Roger left for work about 10pm. As his car rounded the bend, the telephone rang. 'Did you hear the concert?' asked the Bandsman. 'Can I bring my whisky round?'

Pigs weighed deferred gratification against striking while the iron was hot. The whisky won. 'I am very tired; for half an hour, unless you want to leave it till tomorrow,' she said. She had time to fix her eyes – she wore, habitually, at least twice the reasonable amount of eye make-up – and to wash two glasses and set them on coasters. The Bandsman sat at her kitchen table: *his feet under the table, literally,* thought Pigs.

'I'm afraid you had rather a trying time last night,' the Bandsman began.

'It had its moments.'

'Rhythm is so important.'

'So is knowing the tune.'

'That is arguable,' replied the Bandsman. 'I'm afraid my position is not that of first violin, let alone conductor. But I can assure you that the tambourine taps you may be asked to provide will be as important, if less frequent, than the music of other members of the orchestra.'

Pigs was horribly pleased with herself that such an esoteric conversation should take place in her kitchen. *At least I can settle the small things,* she thought, and asked: 'What instrument do you play?'

'Violin for pleasure; in the band, cello.'

'But that couldn't have been a cello you put in your car.'

'No; I play very occasionally in the band, and borrowed. I had been showing off my violin, which is reasonably rare.'

Pigs wondered how far she should push; she thought he had not lied so far; one could get a small arsenal or a large drugs fortune in a violin case.

'Would you like some left-over curry?'

'I should, if you'll join me.'

Occupied with the dishes and microwave, Pigs rather congratulated herself on strategy so far. Over the remains of curry and whisky they established a meeting place and time for next Sunday. This time it was the Bandsman who rang for a lift home. The driver, whether taxi, friend or relative did not come into the house and the car, as Pigs saw when she waved the Bandsman off, had no telephone number emblazoned on its side. Very sleepy, Pigs postponed sleuthing in favour of a good night's sleep.

Arrived home, the Bandsman showered and belched whisky appreciatively. He also slept well. At noon the next day he got back in his car, ensured the violin case was in the boot and went to meet his Chief. Their meeting was satisfactory to both.

'So I can go ahead and recruit her on Sunday,' summarised the Bandsman, 'and the others are paid off.'

'That's right,' agreed the Chief. 'She showed up well to the police questioning and the flat search meantime confirmed our assessment. Her debts are beyond her ability to repay. Her son is the only near relative and the reports from his security firm are good. The dope will provide a useful handle if we ever need one. No need to tell you to keep your head, and she's hardly Mata Hari. Next Sunday, then, and report as normal next week.'

They went to the concert by train. Pigs was pleased about this, her preferred mode of travel. She had never lost the childhood fear of failing to find a lavatory in case of need, and trains were likely to be better equipped. The green and pleasant shimmered through the windows and the carriage was warm almost to the point of discomfort. Also sticky was the walk through London, another favourite Pigs pastime, to the Albert Hall. At the base of the auditorium, they joined the mixed bunch of obvious, score-bearing music lovers and seemingly accidental campers, who lay on kitbags, or sat crossed-legged in Buddhist calm. Pigs enjoyed the varied concert, although the Bandsman was caustically critical of much of the content and some of the performance.

On the way home, they discussed favourite novels. The Bandsman claimed *Travels with My Aunt*, although Pigs opined that somehow it failed to work.

'Brighton is an indefensible first choice for adventure nowadays,' said the Bondsman, 'but Boulogne still has possibilities. What do you say to next weekend?'

A sucker for trips and a Francophile, Pigs was expeditious in agreement and arrangements. She made it so easy that the Bandsman decided to postpone his recruiting until Gauloise, petit café and wine could be adduced in his favour.

Boulogne

The first sight that met Pigs' eyes in Boulogne was a pair of drunk, wild, British men of the type first noted by Julius Caesar, slurping goldwater and exploring both latitude and longitude in their progress. Distressed, Pigs and the Bandsman jumped a taxi, the Bandsman asking for the Palais de Justice in the Haute Ville. There were several cafés opposite, some still with luncheon tables laid. They sat, and ordered, Pigs appeased and her curiosity lulled by the spectacle of the cathedral dome balanced, seemingly, on the roofs. She indulged a fascination with the Bandsman's mouth. This was unusually curved, both altogether and in its component full lower lip and the two semi-arches of the top lip. Pigs remembered reading in girlhood magazines that the way to get your boyfriend to kiss you was to gaze into his eyes and then transfer your attention to his lips. She was just wondering whether this procedure would really have an effect when the Bandsman began his explanations.

'I am involved,' said the Bandsman, 'with an organisation which tries to trace operators in illegal, international organisations. We thought you might help with one such, tracking dealers in child pornography. We have been quite successful watching the usual routes, and have had someone on the channel tunnel run since it started. But we have no-one based in Boulogne, who could watch the people who get off the train and ferry. We rather thought you might fit the bill.'

Now, on the subject of pornography, Pigs was right there on firm ground with those feminists typified by Andrea Dworkin – zero tolerance. She understood the logic of the counter argument; she generally opposed censorship, asserted women's sexual autonomy and saw that sex-play could contest heteropatriarchal models of women's behaviour; but when she envisaged the participants, children, mature, working class, white and black women, underpaid, casual workers, Pigs was up there, shoulder to shoulder with Dworkin. Pigs had questioned how far her own, regretted celibacy inspired her opinions; and had not merely read, but debated the issue, including an infamous, acrimonious session at her local women's group. The latter occasion was one of the factors in her present political inactivity. Pigs had revelled in the warmth of the Women's Movement of her youth; been dismayed at its collapse into dissent; felt the chill as she aged and her opponents in debate seemed slimmer, more fashionable and critical of her eye make-up and the corkscrew curls (though she had not, like Maud in *Possession*, taken to wearing a turban: Pigs could be fierce). Accepting space selling had lost her some of her more politically correct women friends; living with her son ruled out others. Her celibacy restricted conversation. All of these things, and menopausal weariness, had made a period of political quiet attractive. Hence her present foray into writing and sleuthing.

Pigs therefore had time, space and inclination to engage in the Bandsman's scheme. It seemed to involve a prolonged stay in Boulogne, appealing to one who had not been able to afford the smallest holiday for a couple of years; perhaps a chance to reach base camp at Debt mountain. It would be an exaggeration to say that Pigs carefully thought through these things before she agreed, rather, her thoughts flitted to and fro, alighting most often at Debt Base Camp, and frequently on French food and bars. Her reply indicated the style of this flit: 'What's the pay? Do I get expenses? Do I stay in Boulogne? How long for?'

These matters satisfactorily answered, Pigs and the Bandsman traversed the impressive portals of the Palais de Justice. Inside, this was clean, with wide, sweeping staircases. It was nevertheless pervaded with the smell and ambience of the poky, green and distempered corridors of the British magistrates' courts in which Pigs had spent hours with Roger in his cannabis-smoking-young-revelling days: a feeling of cells beneath, containing aeons of boredom laced with menace, waiting to engulf her. Pigs and the Bandsman were made much of, shown the courtrooms and taken into narrow, busy, officious back rooms. The situation was explained to Pigs in detail, maps and diagrams given her plus a reasonably good tourist map which she could be seen to consult whilst she familiarised herself with the town. It was suggested that, during this process, she spend some weeks in a hotel, as a holidaymaker and then bought clothes, had her hair cut French style and moved into an apartment block and made a bid for anonymity.

Correctly interpreting the glaze clouding Pigs eyes, the Bandsman brought the session to an end. They left and took a Thomas Tank look-alike tourist train down the hill and out to the beach. Pigs made straight for her own expanse of wind-cleansed, but hot sand while the Bandsman went into the Nausica centre to telephone. As he had spoken of rejoining her in a couple of hours, Pigs stripped to tee shirt and knickers, then bra-and-knickers and finally knickers alone. She dozed, exposing front, both sides and back in turn, believing that the more she looked brown, the less she looked round. Just as a small espresso became a necessity and she had replaced her clothes, the Bandsman reappeared and they crossed the wide street to an umbrella-shaded café. Pigs was instantly revived by the sense, if not the fact, of bustle so often present in a French café; she pondered this for a while. The clientele was mostly seated and quiet; but there was something definite in the way people turned pages, occasionally ordered, rapped coins, drank, stirred coffee, smoked, exchanged remarks, checked children with minimal effort that promised Happenings; an air of expectancy yet absorption in the moment. She was about to expound on this at length to the Bandsman when, fascinated, she realised that he also was movementé, looking at his watch, catching the waiter's eye.

'We'd better establish you in your hotel, then I must get the next ferry,' he said.

Pigs felt sixteen and friendless. She followed him along the boulevard, back towards embarkation and, with adolescent insistency refused his choice of hotel. She picked one that was adorned by a large, friendly, fairground-mangy dog. The Bandsman arranged a week's accommodation, propelled her to a seat opposite, amongst the now closed mussel and fish stalls, and put a reassuringly large bundle of Euros in her handbag. He made her memorise his telephone number. The Bandsman's obvious concern and reluctance to go calmed Pigs and she was able to see him off in a relatively mature manner; they swapped Gallic kisses to the cheek.

Disobeying explicit orders, Pigs wrote the Bandsman's number down on several scraps of paper which she distributed in separate sections of her handbag. She trailed across the road and climbed the stairs to her new home. From her balcony in a slightly grimy room, Pigs watched the ferry amble away down the narrow channel to the sea. It was extremely hot; she showered, dozed, changed and went to eat.

Back on the balcony she counted the money; it amounted to six months' normal wages. Fishing boats were leaving, tourists chatting, the hotel dog flopped on the pavement below. Fishing lights, neon advertisements, naphtha flares, stars and moon, headlights from constant traffic rebounded, as if the sky was an ever-open French café.

'Oh God of the Debt Mountain,' Pigs told the moon, 'have I got news for you.'

DM had no intention of letting Pigs get away with such frivolity and called Pigs insistently through the night. As she had done rather well with wine and a defiant cognac, she resisted Him until the small hours. Then she spent twenty irritating minutes, removing the money from its hiding place under her pillow, finding several better hiding places around the room, changing her mind, counting and recounting. She wondered if she could open a bank account to deposit her funds without a permanent address; it was not the sort of hotel to keep guests' money in a safe. Indeed, in common with many French bars, the staff had a fine, carefree attitude towards the till and a tendency to wander off to promenade leaving till and customers unattended. Finally, Pigs went on guard on the balcony again and watched the mussel stalls being set up and the fishing boats coming in. She would thus have been perfectly placed to watch the first ferry unload but finally slept, on the balcony, in pyjamas, in the rising sun, handbag, credit cards, Euros and scraps bearing the Bandsman's number scattered around her.

Breakfast, deciding the ratio of bread to croissant to be eaten, was immensely cheering. One woman was washing the bar floor; the chef was bringing up desserts, plated or bowled, to the fridge; the radio played. The first day-trippers were taking up position outside. The chef presented her with the gift of a tall glass of fresh orange juice and Pigs managed a brief conversation. She found it was market day and went purposively into town. It had occurred to her that she could have an interview with a bank manager and explain the position, that she was looking for a flat but had none yet. It remained to chose the bank. She decided on the Credit Agricole, which sounded the cosier of those she considered and where she was received pleasantly. The majority of her money was deposited and she could call for a carnet of cheques the next day. Still with a sizeable fortune in her handbag, Pigs set off to inspect the market. She installed herself in a bar in the square, ordered hot chocolate and watched the crowd. Some tourists and day-trippers were already hunting lunch; again, it was easy to Spot the Brits, who sidled up to the menus and clustered round them but were incapable of choosing a restaurant. It occurred to her that this was a good place for sleuthing; if she watched the boat unload and then came to the square, she would be able to dismiss many of the passengers. She was looking for DVDS, videos, wallets of photographs, and/or a traveller carrying a sizeable amount of hand baggage bearing quantities of these. Many of the smart hotels were also in the square; she could watch people juggling their luggage and registering. Pigs flirted with the market for a bit, bought a local newspaper and tried a second bar. Many of the Brits were still arguing over the menus, getting weary. Already they carried vast amounts of packages. Pigs decided she would have to earn her money, a cheering thought, making her feel busy and important.

By the end of the two weeks Pigs was a dab hand at Boulogne seafront and centre. She knew front and back streets, the times to expect major influxes and lesser straggles of tourists, the bars that stayed resolutely French; she had a passing acquaintance with several waiters, bar owners, and shopkeepers; with the chef at her hotel she was on terms of intimacy. She had devoted a few afternoons to turning and bronzing, now in a smart swimsuit, and had inspected the Haute Ville. She was able to move into a reasonable apartment, with telephone, which caught the sun in the afternoon and boasted a balcony big enough for a chair. Moreover, she had effected a considerable transformation. Regular meals and energetic sleuthing had remoulded her from round to ovaloid; she had a smart new haircut, en brosse; flattering clothes; in a good light, the general impression was chic. These fripperies, plus rent in advance, had made a large hole in her new wealth, but she had sent off receipts for reimbursement. Of pornographic material there had been no clues.

Instruction took the place of deduction. She was to meet the Bandsman from the ferry and help watch the man he would immediately follow. This she did, responding to his effusive greeting and propelling arm so that chattering they pursued their quarry to the Market Square. Pigs was able to commandeer a table that gave sight of the hotel which Quarry entered and ordered drinks from a waiter she could name, to her intense satisfaction and the Bandsman's approbation. Quarry had been distinguished by a big travelling bag and shortly emerged with one much smaller. Pigs was told to follow him, while the Bandsman searched the hotel. For the first time she was afraid. She stomped along behind Quarry, continuing past when he went into a tabac, which she marked. Looking at the plate glass windows that lined either side of the street, she saw Quarry emerge and make his way towards the main street that led to the front. Taking a chance, Pigs carried on a bloc and emerged at the front by her old hotel, so that she and Quarry had each walked two sides of a square. She saw him head back to embarkation and returned to her apartment. Using her binoculars, she was reasonably certain she saw him on deck half-an-hour later. She raced back to the rendezvous with the Bandsman. He had located the original travelling bag in the hotel lockers and found the expected pornography. While they dined, the tabac was raided and found to have both an unusually large sum in the till and the key to the hotel locker. Pigs' first real sleuth had proved a considerable success.

Dinner over, it seemed churlish not to ask the Bondsman back for coffee and cognac. Cognac over, it seemed boorish not to offer him a bed. When he appeared, in bluestriped, old fashioned pyjamas, hesitant, at her bedroom door, it seemed only civil to ask him into her bed. Also, she had her make-up on still, had brushed her teeth and applied perfume. Pigs much enjoyed what followed, after the initial embarrassment, inescapable to one of her generation, of getting into location. Why it should be embarrassing to undress, but not to fuck, she had often asked herself, but not for several years. She was surprised to find how well she remembered the moves, and that she was only slightly dry. Lying underneath and largely inactive, which she preferred, she luxuriated in pleasure.

Also to her taste, Pigs woke alone in the apartment and took a long morning bath. She felt go-o-o-d. As she towelled her newly spiky hair, naked under a slinky dressing gown, flowers arrived from the Bandsman. The deliveryman she slightly knew, from one of the firmly-French bars. She offered him coffee. He offered to arrange the flowers while it brewed. Pigs had not let the bathwater out; he went to get water for the flowers and called her into the steamy, scented, tiled bathroom. Pigs decided afterwards that the only word for what followed was romp. The coffee boiled over and he cleaned it up and did arrange the flowers, to perfection. Then they tried her bed, still unmade. Then, laughing, she insisted he left. He was much too young and energetic; she infinitely preferred the attentions of the Bandsman; but she felt happy, generous, the cat with the cream, Pooh Bear with the honey. After he left she walked to the shore and watched the sea complacently. Intimations of guilt, shame, the Bandsman's disapproval hovered at the edge of her consciousness but she refused to give them room to flourish. Guilt and shame were old foes, analysed in her women's group, debated with friends, the theme of many novels. Pigs had her answers ready to attacks from such quarters, would assert her right to pleasure and the importance of her self-interest. Most disconcerting was her fear of the Bandsman's disapproval. Pigs preferred not to think about the implications of this emotion. She thought, *I could have filmed it and arrested myself.*

Christ, thought Pigs, *film,* thought Pigs, *fool, idiot, stomping, crashing catastrophe of a woman.* The ferry surged out, the waving trippers mocking her. She had once seen Flowerman in the raided *tabac. I'm Watson when I ought to be Holmes; he was using me, checking me out, I'll go back to space-selling.* Rage pervaded her skin and head like a menopausal flush. She determined to confront Flowerman and marched straight to his usual café. He was there, his face lit up on seeing her and he immediately joined her and ordered drinks. He asked to walk her home, desisted when she invented a shopping trip, escorted her to the door.

Pigs was flummoxed. She had never realised before how complex was the life of a spy. The last ten minutes had been amongst the most difficult she had negotiated. Anger had vanished completely at his greeting. On her own account, she had no intention of repeating the escapade and would have preferred a couple of months of evasion followed by distant courtesy. On account of her job, she needed to assess whether Flowerman was in any way genuine, or trying to subvert her loyalty/search her apartment/plant material/

19

establish her sexual attitudes/find out about the Bandsman... she raced back to the apartment to see how it felt, what its ambience told her. She sorted through two days' post for clues. There were nasty letters from Visa companies. Debt Mountain had not budged. Pigs, old, tired, bloated, wept into her second bath: *I can't even go on the game now... I'm already on it.*

The telephone rang. A huddled and dripping Pigs answered and was immensely cheered by the Bandsman's voice. He told her that Quarry had been followed to a London address and several arrests had been made. Although he omitted to tell her about his carpeting for having endangered both of them (confession to his Boss being so automatic and essential for survival that he had never considered hiding any of the details surrounding his visit) she caught the anxiety in his tone and was flattered. Her instructions were to carry on as normal. He was sending reimbursement for the apartment. Pigs was tempted to tell him about the Visa letters but did not, in case it sounded as if she was asking for money for services rendered. However, restored, she dressed, starting with her best strawberry-design-and-white satin knickers and went to award herself a meal served by her friendly chef. She cuddled the dog. *It was fun*, she thought with the entrée. By desert, she wore a smutty grin. *Thank God I'm in my forties, not my twenties*, and finally, after careful consideration of the finer details over coffee, *I'm POST menopausal.*

The morning, like Southern trees, bore a strange fruit: dead flower heads in a gift parcel with pornographic pictures of a child. Pigs was devastated by disgust and fear, compassion and anger. Her memories of Roger at the same age as the child in the photographs leapt sharply into focus, overlaying the print. Pigs forced herself to try to see what was erotic about the photographs, to try to understand a voyeur who could find pleasure in this vulnerability. She found most obscene the suppressed power of the man glimpsed as an outline, offstage – obscure but heavily felt, as was most power. The man derived his power from being unseen, from rendering visible the tortured boy, from the control his freedom to move beyond the light gave him, from the hands skeletal in outline which had just inflicted, might renew, horrors that were left to the imagination. The erotic imagination, she supposed. The chains that confined the boy were redundant; it was his own fear, his slightness that attracted the light of his martyrdom. Worst of all, the child smiled. Could anyone believe that smile?

The single resolution Pigs could usefully make, and she took it instantly, was to put more effort into catching the dealers. Anyone behaving in an obvious manner was not a major problem: the goldwater drunks flashing photographs and giggling, the DVD bought for cash on the fringes of the market, transferring from inside pocket to inside pocket she could and did spot and in several instances a traveller found himself inside the Palais de Justice. But the traveller did not reveal the supplier because he did not know him; a furtive exchange at the ferry bar, a message to be left at a certain café, were fairly freely offered up to the police but were insufficiently specific. Yet that boy had been abused because photographs, such as those delivered to her, sold for cash. The pleasure of the voyeur was used to justify the assault. How to stop this? The change-the-world, challenge-the-pleasure approach she had tried in several women's groups had been partly successful; abusive paedophiles running children's homes and hospital wards had been revealed in the new climate. The Bandsman's way, and Pigs had always seen its attractions, was to stop the trade, or make it too expensive to operate. Pigs' mental eye fixed on the dead flowers, rather than the photographs; perhaps she could be an *agent provocateur*.

Pondering these problems, Pigs made up her eyes, tidied the flat and went to the very busy café one fell into if walking in a straight line from ferry disembarkation. As usual at this time in the morning, which in England she would have called elevenses, the clientele was mixed. A man of perhaps gipsy descent, swarthy with long black curls and a sharp, pearl grey suit, was sipping espressos with a well-fed, clean businessman. The waiters, in capacious aprons, were beginning to lay places for lunch. There was a mezzanine floor from which one could see the whole of the ground floor and here Pigs established herself with a hot chocolate. A thought had come to her on her journey to the café, come and taken possession. Despite her good vantage point it obscured her vision. She was already an *agent provocateur*. That was why she, so inexperienced, so bullish, so roundly noticeable, had been chosen. It came from wearing strawberry knickers. The Bandsman must have been expecting the dealers to attack her. They had, but in such a way that she could not tell him about it. She had been warned.

Pigs tried to work out what had governed her response to the Bandsman. She remembered a one-time prospective lover who, deep in his own shell of fears and morbid memories, never quite came to the point. Gently, gently their romance had grown, never quite a love affair, understated, arms-length, deriving from this a huge erotic charge. That man had been quizzical, witty, caustic, rather like the Bandsman. Several times the affair that had never been an affair had seemed about to peter out, and then revived itself, in the turn of a head, the flame of a lighter. He had been younger than she but somehow both more used by and less involved in life. Class, she had decided, was a factor; she remembered the Dory Previn song about the cool, middle class man who hurt her more than the straightforward, rougher worker. This man never wept, never laughed, drank and ate with restraint, remained controlled. Sometimes she had felt his eyes on her and had never been sure whether their gaze was one of enquiry, concern or contempt – perhaps surprise. Their small budget of shared kisses she had treasured, would treasure still, but their perfection had rendered any aftermath redundant. Fidgety, preoccupied, he had held himself aloof and yet their relationship had survived, in fits and starts, with nips and tucks, until she followed the Bandsman. It was in her now, that searching, questing relationship. Pigs would have preferred Flowerman in her thoughts, for all his attendant problems. But this other lingered, and his resemblance to the Bandsman disturbed her; had she carried straight on, from a phase the Bandsman had not known her to have reached? Was this latter relationship the fulfilment of the earlier, so that she had skipped necessary growths in their understanding?

So she must deal alone with her warning. Pigs picked from the small vase on the table a bloom that had withered and pinned it in her buttonhole. She felt disoriented, vacuous and very cold. In the lavatory she perfected her make up. Then she braved Flowerman's café. She was politely served, exchanged a few words, drank her coffee, left the dead flower with the tip and left. Still cold and vacant, she fetched her towel, changed into her swimsuit and went to turn and bronze. The ferry trundled in; she firmly shut her eyes, making slits that she could have used to encourage the circus lions. She felt the lions were round about. But she could not shut out the image of the chained boy.

Paris

The following day, Roger telephoned to tell Pigs that his security firm wanted him to work full-time in Hamburg. Trained by Pigs to travel by the cheapest route, he had taken advantage of a Eurostar special offer that would land him in Paris, en route, in a couple of days. He would like to see Pigs. They arranged to meet at the Gare du Nord. Guilty at burdening him, Pigs told Roger about the Visa bills. Roger had his first month's wages in advance and offered to make payments; Pigs could repay him in Euros. Pigs' spirits rose measurably. Soon after, the Bandsman rang and approved the Paris trip, so long as Pigs was in Boulogne to meet the weekend ferries. Excited, Pigs booked herself into a cheap hotel in the Marais, planning to scoot round some favourite haunts when she had seen Roger off to Hamburg. She drew out the sizeable amount of money needed to recompense Roger.

Pigs took an old, slow train to Paris. Her maternal enthusiasm on meeting Roger was slightly dimmed by two things. First, Roger was accompanied not by the current embodiment of his longstanding ideal of female beauty, wraith-like, fair-haired and silent, but by a vocal, round, dark, in short Pigs-like creature. Second, someone very like the Flowerman was lingering in the crowd. Both these distractions were, however, easily overcome by Roger's news that he had sold some of Pigs' furniture and china and actually cleared one of the Visa bills. Pigs danced. Non-wraith-like kissed her warmly. They all went to the café immediately opposite the station, where Pigs was allowed to order the food and wine, having promised Roger to pay in cash. It was a happy occasion; steamy, noisy, peopled by constant ingresses and egresses of customers; it could not possibly be Flowerman a few booths away. On the other hand, one always knew, if someone one had slept with was near.

Having said goodbye to Roger and Non-wraith, Pigs ambled down the rue du Rivoli towards her dingy hotel. Once restored in a corner café, she revisited the antique shops of the Village de Saint Paul, then paid her dues to the Seine and the locksmith's museum, which had delighted a young Roger. In the Picasso museum she mused on the Centaur; like Flowerman, he was playful, evasive, half threat, half wild joke, and omnipresent round each corner. Arriving at her hotel and disliking its tiny lift, she huffed up the winding staircase by which it was encased. On the threshold of a room that hardly merited the name, she was abruptly stopped by the sight of a violin case just inside the door. The Bandsman smiled at her.

'How did you know...?' began Pigs.

'It is, after all, my job.'

Sometime later, rosy with the evidence of his still-enthusiastic attentions, Pigs attempted to obtain more information. She was forestalled by the Bandsman's asking whether she had spotted anyone from Boulogne at the station. 'Maybe,' conceded Pigs, determined to die horribly rather than admit to romps bathroom and bedroom. She described Flowerman. Under further interrogation, she outlined the Visa card/cash deal. For the first time since she had met him, the Bandsman appeared exasperated.

'Why didn't you tell me?' he asked.

'I couldn't.'

'Next time,' said the Bandsman, revealing a wholly accurate assessment of Pig's financial acumen, 'you can. Do you realise it will look as if you have been laundering money?'

Pigs was contrite.

'Perhaps it will force their hand,' the Bandsman relented.

'What's in your violin case?' countered Pigs.

He showed her. Money. Heaps of money. Pigs was appalled, trying to estimate its worth in overdrawn Visa cards. Debt Mountain god would have bowed before it. She went over and sat by it, felt it, took some out, piled it up. The Bandsman got up and was brisk about washing and dressing.

'I'm going away for a bit,' he said.

Pigs heard him in her stomach, in her rising gorge. She was silenced, blanched.

'Is it because...?'

'No, no no,' he assured her, 'it was already arranged, that's what the money's for.'

He cuddled and petted her. The surer she felt of his regard, the more Pigs feared.

'Its dinner time,' he said at length. 'I should perhaps have mentioned that you also have a journey. We meet in Amsterdam in a few weeks.'

'I don't wa-a-a-ant to go to Amsterdam,' Pigs wailed.

'You will, by the time you get off the train.'

Pigs chuckled. 'Oh, but it had better be a good dinner.'

'We are in Paris.'

'I love you,' Pigs said.

'I rather think the feeling's mutual.'

'Oh my God.'

' – and all the gods. Lets make oblation. Champagne in the Champs Élysées?'

Pigs saw he was laughing and crying. Her fear increased, smote her breasts, made her genitals ache. With her fear grew her courage. A befuddled and bedraggled Pigs saw him off a few hours later. *My day for goodbyes,* she thought. On the other side of the platform was Flowerman.

By superhuman effort, Pigs prevented herself from waving, but she could not bear the idea of being followed, the sound of pursuing feet back to the hotel. She walked into the metro opening, intending to escape into the side street, but found the dark space uninviting and swept back into the light. An ill-favoured, ill-dressed, elderly man with gold teeth mounted in dingy plaque accosted her, grinning and gesticulating. 'Va - t- en,' hissed Pigs, and he did, like an evanescent fairground vision in a hall of mirrors. Encouraged, Pigs made for the taxi queue; she was lucky, and soon reached the hotel. There, the tumbled bed soothed her, as did some roses that had appeared on the little apology of a desk. She was settling for the night when she realised the violin case was still in the room: disaster. Pigs wrenched the violin case open; it was empty. Multitudinous symptoms of poor digestion spontaneously returned. Pigs beat her head with her hands. If the money had been stolen, she wished she had been the thief and paid her debts. Perhaps the Bandsman would die for want of it. Perhaps she would be accused of treason, arrested by the French police, and Maigret must have retired. The waiter knocked with a balloon glass of brandy and a note from the Bandsman: *'Everything's ok – no worries – enjoy the roses – love...'*

It must be ok, it must, it must, thought Pigs. She checked the bolts on the window, wrapped the bedspread round her and squatted on the rug by the door, cradling her body. She would not be killed in her bed.

As dawn rose, pale lemon, Pigs woke and some of her ebullience returned. She liked Amsterdam; several trips with an adolescent Roger had contributed to Debt Mountain. And she would need new clothes. Turning-and-bronzing days were by no means over, but had become a bonus; for Amsterdam she would need a jacket. And night things, of course. And a case; or bag, nobody had a case nowadays. She breakfasted in her corner café, where the waiter's voice approached her, filling the space before him. He was lean and spare, not unlike the Bandsman, but obviously owed some of his genes to rural forbears; he had the thick shoulders massing from his neck, although his chest was elongated, pinched, and he was grey with indoor life. She spent the morning and early afternoon as tourist. At the Palais Royal gardens, so formal and contained, the spindly iron seats hosted their usual mix of meditative Parisians and half-bewildered, swollen-ankled strangers; the horses of the Arc de Triomphe des Carousels caught the light as always, gleaming gold. Notre Dame des Victoires ignored the apology on the wall of the building opposite, from which the Vichy regime had run anti-Semitic programmes. The little Rue Bonaparte spilt her out at St Germain des Pres. Pigs caught a bus and the slow train back to Boulogne, a rose in her buttonhole.

Pigs remained in Boulogne for a month. She had some success; experienced by now in spotting unusual travellers, she reported on several who were found interesting by Customs. Then she got word that the period in which she could reasonably be expected to remain useful in Boulogne was expiring but that she was wanted in Amsterdam. A large sum of money was credited to her English bank account and Pigs managed to clear another Access card. This would have pleased her greatly just two months ago but now meant surprisingly little. Pigs decided on a final visit to her friendly chef: the evenings were getting chilly for eating outside and she was enticed to the upstairs restaurant. She had a good place by the window. From it, she saw one of Flowerman's copains and she saw, meeting him, a man carrying a large suitcase. She asked to use the chef's telephone and contacted an emergency number she had been given for the Hotel de Ville. She found there was another Watcher, who had already reported, and stomped back to her cooling moules. As she bent forward to seat herself, copain looked straight up into her eyes. Pigs' appetite might have vanished, but she could not disappoint Chef on her last day.

Amsterdam

En route for Amsterdam, Pigs' alarms were allayed by the exit from Boulogne, the new coat in the luggage rack and the rose now in her buttonhole, presented by a total stranger at the Gare du Nord, with the Bandsman's compliments. She peered at Brussels and began to feel quite chirpy when that stage-post was passed. The familiar sweep of the boulevard from Amsterdam Centraal Station, plus the financial ability to hire a taxi, cheered her. Her hotel was in a quiet, tree-lined street near the Concertgebouw and the café/bodega on the corner was an old haunt: dark-red Second Empire, decorated with Art Nouveau lampshades and giant palms in brown-black pots, shut safely from the street by heavy curtains on brass poles. Musicians came in, smart concertgoers. Whereas the French swooped on a café like swallows, sang to each other all at once and flew off, the Dutch gathered more like the herons from the Artis zoo, stately, silent, purposeful, but also restless. There were more flowers in Pigs' room. Given the constraints of space in this city, where the buildings were like tall ships jostling in a harbour, Pigs' habitation was not much bigger than those into which she and Roger had once squeezed, but its fittings were infinitely superior. Pigs equipped herself with a ticket for the concert and ate afterwards. Post-Boulogne, the food was a disappointment, but one which Pigs felt she could bear in exchange for the absence of Flowerman. *Fancy coming to Amsterdam to get away from sex,* Pigs thought.

    The following morning, Pigs made her way to the café that was the venue for her assignation with the Bandsman. He was there; and she could hardly bear the lift of her heart, the lightness of her being, the fanfare in her head, the shine of her own regard that lit him as would a spotlight. Equally appalling and enthralling was the light he cast on her; but warned by his manner, her greeting was decorous. She nodded, as to a distant friend; she ordered her own coffee. Instructions were simple; to minutely examine the dossier he would leave, removing it in the large bag she had been told to provide. This was easily accomplished and she watched him leave, giving him ten minutes before facing the varied seediness of the tacky kitsch and genuine antiques in Waterlooplein. Once she had half-planned to make her fortune by importing antique exotic dolls and other reminders of the Dutch East Indies but the trade seemed sullied by its past. Pretend Native American ware was popular this year and modern, wooden witches on broomsticks. Mason's ironstone china masqueraded as Delft. Some of the nineteen-sixties clothing appealed strongly to Pigs but was not appropriate for her post-Boulogne character. Instead, she bargained aggressively for a silver, violin shaped lighter for the Bandsman. Too pleased and excited to return to the hotel, despite the weight of the file she carried, Pigs walked through the old Jewish quarter to Artis, paid the exorbitant entrance fee and went to watch the herons swoop, rise, dip, settle. They gathered in a darkish, tree-surrounded pool, hovering over earth-bound, angry storks, the whole reminiscent of a Tolkein scene. Her heart rose with the skybound herons, which eased swiftly to a higher branch, gracefully and proudly alighting on new territory. The storks, anchored to the grass, flapped and called.

Pigs had more coffee in a restaurant beside the flamingo lake and began on the file. It contained computer-scanned pictures and text on hundreds of people. The pictures all looked alike until she got her eye in. She felt the Bandsman's presence as she worked, through his link to the file; she also felt his absence. She fingered the pages. She was to pick out anyone, anyone at all whom she recognised. Soon her eyes ached. She left and jumped a tram back to her hotel, opened her window and sat at the desk before it, concentrating on her file. She made a short list of possibilities and narrowed it down to three probables. She copied out the details of these three and made sketches of them, placing the pages between the leaves of a book. She went down to dinner.

The Bandsman joined her when she had got to the tiramisu. Pigs felt now a security in his presence, even when danger flew like herons all about them. He was a bit like a heron – lean, long-necked, darkish, concentrated, ready to soar or swoop. As she passed him the book, he smiled. He went to the lavatory and when he came back returned the book. He said, well done. He asked her to suggest a lunch venue for the morrow, she named the café/bodega. He kissed her hand, but not her lips and left. Pigs felt that she was not quite satisfied, not quite safe, not quite wholly beloved. But life was definitely worth living. She ordered brandy, not the second rate French she would get if she requested cognac, but Dutch brandy, sweeter and smoother, for lingering over. She lingered. The she went to lay awake in her cell, to sigh, to ponder.

Things did not improve the next morning when a hand-delivered message cancelled the bodega meeting. Pigs would have liked to hear the Bandsman's voice, the better to judge the meaning of the message. She decided on action. A canal boat was out of the question. Too much water. Pigs had internalised, despite herself, an Anita Brookner novel set partly in Venice, in which water symbolised despair, the nagging drainage of frustration, the stench of lost hopes. Café-bouncing was the obvious remedy. Pigs applied lashings of make-up and her best clothes to her bruised spirits and set forth. The weather, at first heavy, settled into brightest blue, the canals responded, flits of shimmering pale grey spicing the blue, houses distinguished themselves from their neighbours in the light, people gathered. Avoiding the main streets, Rokin, Leidsestraat, Pigs traversed Prinsengracht and Kaisergracht in the cool, decayed grandeur of the outer-centre zone. *Today I am free,* she thought, *suspended, alone.* She tried some of the speciality shops, bought cigarette papers in exotic packages, entered antique shops and fingered the wood, sumptuous in its age, slightly oily beneath her fingers. A saxophone reminded her of a night in an Amsterdam jazz club. The saxophone player in his snazzy jacket had been proud of his trumpeter daughter. A young woman with straight blonde hair and pouting lips, like the early Brigitte Bardot, swerving her body in its black trousers and shiny tee shirt to the exertions of her deep breaths, she blew notes from her stomach. She was the darling of the club and had revelled in its adoration, punching the air, laughing. Pigs hesitated over a miniature saxophone. She realised there was a waiting to be done.

As she wandered and waited, to Pigs' joy she was on the bridge over the Amstel when it opened to let through a boat, the lifting arm of the bridge beckoning her up and out of time. She carried on to Hortus Botannicus. That a bright drizzle was beginning to damp out the blue of the sky rather added to her pleasure in renewing acquaintance with the ordered plants, the cork walks, the tidy clipped hedges. The paths sparkled; plops of sound indicated pools forming.

Pigs wended her way to the fern house where she had once measured Roger against the bark and fingered the spiky stems around his head. The fronds now splintered her view; she felt overlooked. A watcher would see her entire while she would see green zebra patterns in all directions. A man with combat fatigues on zebra limbs was near; Pigs abandoned her intention of climbing up to the tiny gallery that surmounted the ferns and quickly slid a door that led to the river. The man followed. Pigs paused by the bee tree-hive. DO NOT TOUCH was the legend, DO NOT DISTURB THE BEES YOU MAY BE STUNG. The man overtook her and stood easily, blocking her path, smiling. He had sallow skin. Pigs doubled back, back through the sliding door, but the man outside paced smartly to the main entrance. Back again, she left under cover of a family party, ran down the river path to the greenhouse of exotic plants and charged inside. Deciding against several ground floor paths that circled the greenhouse, leading to an inevitable dead-end, Pigs climbed the spindly spiral iron staircase to the glass walk, which gave her a view of all the plants and people below. She was sweaty and growling for breath in the heat. The glass walk wobbled and creaked underfoot and the rain, stronger now, spattered with increased frequency. Sick at heart, Pigs saw the sallow man slide the door. He smiled still. Not trusting her wet shoes on the glass, Pigs proceeded in a fast shuffle across her bridge. The sallow man nimbly leapt up the stairs and seemed to dance after her, light, controlled, purposeful. Pigs shot through the inner door to the hotter, second greenhouse, where insects revelled in the tropical climate. She leant across the door for protection but felt it slide across her shoulders as the man pulled it open. She fell on her knees. The man bent towards her and in desperation Pigs rolled and grabbed his legs. They thudded down together on the small path and she wriggled from him, blessing the family who now entered and were soon engaged in picking the man up, crying out normal sounds of courtesy. Pigs, picking her way through the tropics as though an expert in guerrilla warfare, silently reached the end fire door, not to be opened except in emergency, and let herself out to the cool canal bank. She did not ignore the alarms; rather, she noted them as otherworldly, nothing to do with her. She was thus able to present a front of perfect innocence that proved a satisfactory cover until she had gained the safety of the tearoom in the Jewish Historical Museum.

Pigs sat a long time, trying several of the different flavoured tea sachets from her wicker basket. She returned to her hotel when she felt entirely refreshed, able to run if need be, alert to potential danger signals. At reception there were no messages. A bath, a sleep and a meal she took in silence. No telephone calls. At breakfast, no message. Pigs yearned to tell her tale. She wanted her doubts assuaged, her interpretations justified, medals for bravery. None came. By the third day she was losing sleep and weight. A week went by, Pigs never far from hotel and bodega. The problem with eating alone, she decided, was not, as the Brookner heroine opined, that you ate too early, but that you ate too fast. Unless you fought back the over-attentive waiters, in sixty minutes you were back on the pavement, belly full, head muzzy, a sizeable sum of money lighter. Waiters did not like single females; why should they? It was a question of economics, the woman alone took up the space for two, maybe four diners – one to three less meals paid for and tips given. Once she went to the Waterlooplein café and tried to summon the Bandsman by willpower. Eventually she phoned Roger in Hamburg. Too studiously relaxed, she was immensely relieved when he found her out and suggested a little holiday, a break, a rest. He had a job near the border; he could get to Nijmegen. Roger ordered her onto a train and told her to leave all the arrangements to him, he would book a hotel, they would have a long weekend, he had things to tell her.

Without reporting to her contact number, Pigs boarded the specified train for her weekend, feeling uncomfortably that she was absent without leave, and that this journey was different to the Paris one, when she had sought permission for her trip and then been surprised by the Bandsman's appearance. She felt that a gulf had opened, that she was outside the Bandsman's thoughts, abandoned to play a game she did not understand. Pigs was no good at sports. At her school, team spirit had been encouraged by the games mistress' practice of naming two captains for rounders, who then chose their own teams. Pigs had nearly always been amongst the last few, truly bad performers, huddled in a small and non-expectant group, as the captains picked their way down the ranks of good, moderate and indifferent players. She had felt fat, and flaccid, and smelly, as if she was stagnating. Now, for the first time since her adventures began, Pigs wondered at her lack of knowledge about her role in the Bandsman's team. Who had named the Bandsman? Who was in charge? How would success, a finish to her mission, be accomplished? Was her part in the proceedings sufficient to warrant the sums of money that she had received? Had falling in love with the Bandsman been part of the plot? Had she been duped into quiescence, caressed into discarding normal questions about her task?

The arrival of the trolley with hot water and choice of flavoured tea bags somewhat soothed these questionings. When the train finally crossed the bridge over the Waal, Pigs was able to look out with a renewed sense of eager expectation; she had always been near the start of Roger's team. A working river, the Waal repaid her attention with a view of barges, some pulled and some pushed by their engines, some low in the river and straining. As she walked up the platform she saw Roger; he hugged her and she was struck by the warmth of their mutual regard, the long-standing ease of their relationship. They jumped a taxi to the Waalkade and made for one of the cafés whose tables spread down to the water's edge. The early evening sun shone over the bridge and Pigs' natural sense of well-being reasserted itself. There had, after all, been days when her best friend was named captain and chose Pigs first, first of everyone, for her team. There had even been the very infrequent occasions when Pigs was herself named, although this had made her feel hot and undeserving. And of the few bad players, Pigs had not been quite the worst.

Roger's news was welcome, if somewhat startling. He was marrying the young woman she had met in Paris. He wanted to marry in England, and for Pigs to open up the house so that the reception could range from garden to conservatory to indoors, depending on the weather. Pigs exclaimed, in Mitford-family style, and entered fully into these arrangements. Roger had fixed a weekend at the end of October, giving time for the banns. Pigs would need to get home pretty soon. They walked up through the narrow streets, rebuilt after allied bombing to the original pattern, to the town centre area near the surviving parts of old Nijmegen. They ate in a glass-fronted café, watching the social life of the evening advance. Over coffee Roger asked, gently probing, about Pig's job, about her finances. Pigs felt a great temptation to tell him all about her train-journey doubts, to ask advice, to lean a little. The responsibilities of maternity prevented her from being thoroughly open; but she said enough for Roger to evince concern. Could she book leave; for that matter, how would she leave the job, he wanted to know; would she have to give notice. Pigs had no answer. What most horrified Roger was that Pigs had no idea what her salary was over a given period, or how much of the money that came her way was hers to spend as she liked, without accounting for its destination.

'For all you know,' said Roger, rather severely, 'the money now in your account is meant to last until Christmas.'

'I've paid off a lot of the Visa cards,' Pigs replied, placatingly.

'But you don't know when you'll next get paid – you could easily build them up again. Don't you think you'd better look round for a proper job? See what's going?'

'It is a proper job, it's important, I'm glad to be doing it.'

'Are you telling me everything?'

'No.'

Roger sat back, sighed. Pigs looked mulish, kicking her heels against her chair leg. Their eyes caught and they started to grin at the role reversal, till Roger shouted with laughter. He took her to the hotel he had booked them, and for a final drink to the noisy, spit-and-sawdust bar next door. Pigs loved him to the exclusion of all other emotion. The rest of their weekend was idle, pleasurable, friendly. Pigs was very proud of her son.

Returning to Amsterdam, Pigs felt calmer than she had for several weeks past. It seemed that a crisis had come and gone in her strange job, which she had never really understood. She had survived, reasonably unblemished, physically. In fact she looked forward to showing off the more ovaloid, and elegantly coiffed Pigs. Debt Mountain god had been propitiated. Pigs was aware that he merely slumbered, for, as Roger had suspected, the debit balances were mounting again, but having once smiled on her, DM God had lost his awesomeness. Roger's wedding would be exciting, another epoch passing. The English house and its lifestyle was not an attractive proposition, but she was familiar with its dullness, the weariness of a winter evening spent alone, the cold hush of the night hours. The nub of her slight depression, which kept jostling up against her new-found calm, elbowing it aside for dangerous seconds, was, of course, the Bandsman. Pigs did not even know how to begin thinking about him. As someone past? Passed? A fond remembrance?

Pigs regained the hotel. No post, no telephone messages. She climbed the stairs and fiddled with her key card. On the threshold, she felt apprehensive, her breath came quickly. Pigs marched boldly in. The Bandsman was standing with his back to the room, leaning his hands, his long, delicate, strong fingers, on the windowsill. He was incongruously dressed in her towelling dressing gown. He did not move. Pigs entered, shut and locked the door, threw her bags on the bed and waited. She called his name. Slowly he turned and Pigs yelled out, quickly silenced by the pressure of those fingers. He was covered in blood. It oozed from his shoulder, just below the collar bone. It gushed from cuts on his cheeks and arms. His hands, she saw, were grimed with it. It smeared her face now and made clots on her dressing gown. His penis was sheathed in blood. Calling, calling softly, moaning to him, Pigs caught him in her arms and enveloped him, kissed him. He half-fell down on top of her and they made love, he tearing off Pigs' clothes, urgent, desperate. She washed his penis in the fluid of her vagina, sucked his fingers clean, rubbed blood back into his hair as she hugged him. Satiated, sobbing, they both slept.

He called her when he had run them both a bath. Pigs lay between his legs, her head cradled on the Bandsman's shoulder. He asked her to tell him everything that had happened since their last meeting. Pigs' account of Hortus Botannicus lost nothing in the telling and she was rewarded by the tautness she felt in his arms as she recounted her danger. He chuckled at her escape. Then she told him about Roger, skipping over the waiting week when she had feared him gone. He nibbled her ear. For the first time, Pigs, in her turn, demanded an explanation. He had been called back to England on the day of Pigs' adventure, to go through the files of the shortlist of suspects. Then he had watched Pigs' hotel. Pigs appeared to be behaving impeccably, putting up the perfect tourist front. He had been about to join her at the end of the first day's watching when what he feared had come about; it was obvious that Pigs was being followed. He had waited for her to make contact; she did not. Concerned for her safety, he had resorted to the stratagem of contacting Roger, suggesting the weekend break. Pigs' call to Roger had been a bonus.

Pigs stiffened in his arms when she found that her precious, calm, friendly weekend had been no such thing but a devious plot to get her out of Amsterdam.

'That was you? You did it?' she demanded.

'To keep you safe,' he apologised.

'And Roger? What is this? Male bonding? Is the wedding a plot?'

'Roger was very cross. He bit my head off. Who was I, why was I messing up your life, what were my intentions, what were you getting involved in, how dare I. I had to go to Hamburg to meet him.'

(That's why I heard nothing for a week, thought Pigs, satisfied.)

'We got on together very well,' the Bandsman said. 'I also met you future daughter-in-law. I convinced Roger that my intentions were honourable.'

That was too much for Pigs, lying in the bath in his arms. Her twisting and turning as the Roger plot was related had already begun to effect the Bandsman's libido; Pigs pounced at him, taking him inside her, enjoying him. Then they reran the water and she bathed and anointed him. The only really deep cut was the one below the shoulder, which he had roughly bandaged. Pigs made a more professional job of it. He had come back to the hotel to wait for her and been careless. He had been beaten up in her room, had been cut fending off a knife attack, had been stripped and threatened with castration. Blood from the shoulder wound had been smeared over him to demonstrate the might-have-been and he had been left unconscious. He had just come round and wrapped himself in Pig's dressing gown when she entered. They were no longer safe. They must leave Amsterdam that evening. Pigs' job, as she had suspected, was, in any case complete. He could identify his assailants and that would break one part of the ring. Pigs had been invaluable. Pigs thought that this explanation fell short in many aspects, but as the key area of the Bandman's feelings for her seemed to be established beyond reasonable doubt, she asked no more questions. She did ask

37

him what was to happen to her and, to her surprise, was given a straight answer.

'You go home. You get ready for Roger's wedding. You are debriefed. We pay you a minimum allowance. You keep yourself ready to identify people and photographs, to testify. Later, if you're willing, there might be another job.'

'And you? Do I see you?' she asked.

By now they were dressed, packed and sitting in the bodega. 'Of course you do,' the Bandsman replied, holding her hands. 'I do love you. My intentions are honourable. I want us to have a future, if you do.'

'But do we meet? I mean daily, weekly, monthly?'

'There are things I must do. Trust me. Don't look forlorn. I shan't hurt you. I will make us a future. In which we meet, daily, weekly, monthly.'

Pigs decided, in the circumstances, and because she did feel secure and beloved in his presence, that she would put away the forlorn look and trust to the future. There were little splinters of ice in her whisky, but it was good for all that. It was a great pleasure and comfort to her that they travelled back to England together, like a normal couple, running for the train at Centraal Station, sitting in the bar at Schipol Airport from which one could view the airplanes, showing their passports together, sitting side by side and holding hands for take-off, opening their little plastic box of eats, getting drinks from the trolley. Pigs wanted the flight never to end.

Roger's Wedding

Back home, Pigs brooded. There was nothing she could do but trust the Bandsman. She could not make them out a future, she knew too little about him and his work. If he cared, he would make arrangements; if he did not care, she would have to go without. Pigs hated to be the passive one, not to have the power of decision. She delayed contacting the people of her pre-Bandsman life, not knowing if she would be moving again. However, the preparations for Roger's wedding meant that she had to start picking up the threads. The church was to be local and the reception was to be at Pigs' house, as Roger had asked. Pigs had to correspond with her new daughter-in-law's family, consult their wishes, book them into a hotel. There were several pleasant hours spent at a garden centre, renovating the conservatory. The curry shop was as good as ever. Pigs began not to sleep too well. Her hot flushes had come back, as if showing withdrawal symptoms for the loss of the Bandsman's attentions. Too much sitting in a sorry torpor was rounding her outline. Having placed orders and paid deposits for plants, food, drink, extra chairs, she feared the debts mounting. Her Amsterdam expenses had not come through. It was then that, playing a long shot, a fundamentally ever-hopeful Pigs picked up her early attempts to make her fortune as an author and started to write her adventures.

Waiting for Roger's wedding, despite the many and thousand things to do, the lists to write, Pigs was often gently bored, sometimes quite pleasantly, sometimes on the verge of the Slough of Despond. She re-read her well-thumbed, food and drink stained, stock of Georgette Heyers. This was an indulgence about which she had felt shamefaced for a number of years, and to which she would never have admitted at the women's group; however, it had been sanctioned when she heard on Radio 4 that her appetite for Heyer was shared by A.S. Byatt. In this waiting time, Pigs gave serious attention to her Desert Island discs. She had decided to ask for *Larousse Gastronomique* instead of Shakespeare and her 1930s illustrated *Waverley Dictionary* instead of the Bible. That left her choice of book free – *Winnie the Pooh in Latin*, with a primer? The luxury was difficult; Brian Keenan had chosen a pencil, Dame Judy Dench a map of the world. She decided on a bundle of the little square-lined exercise books she had used while sleuthing in Boulogne. The Bandsman's visits were kingfisher bright darts of light in the quiet pool of these preparatory days. He never betrayed to Pigs that he knew all about Flowerman. It was his secret indulgence, it added spice, bitter, but flavour-enhancing, to his love and lovemaking. Pigs was in a fair way to forgetting the incident, although the arrival of wedding-flowers, cellophane-wrapped, caused a shiver of dread.

Having seemed an immovable obstruction on the horizon, Roger's wedding date suddenly sped forward as if to cheat Pigs of final preparation time. She was rather pleased with her outfit, which she thought showed a cosmopolitan taste, a severely cut grey suit with a long jacket. Roger arrived from Hamburg. Presents were delivered; Pigs enjoyed the wrapping paper and the gift cards. On the wedding day, the conservatory gleamed green and beflowered, the garden paths shone, weed-free, after an early shower. They set off for church arm-in-arm, walking. The bride's family took control, escorted Roger into church and made sure Pigs sat where she should. There was a great flurry of cars and photographs afterwards and then Pigs was racing home to let in the guests. She had done the rounds once with sherry and wine, when she became aware of the ever-sceptical gaze of a familiar and beloved figure. The Bandsman had arrived.

Tom Christmas

Suzannah was flitting around the London gallery, dabbing at pieces of her exhibition, dusting, adjusting, when Tom Christmas spoke to her for the first time. His comical, screwed-up face, bracketed by his big ears, prevented him from appearing threatening, despite his immoderate height and bulk. Suzannah was nevertheless frightened that he would knock against one of her sculptures, or annihilate one of the smaller exhibits, the gnomish figures that she called her Little Men. These brought Suzannah a steady income; she sold them on a market stall every Saturday, although she was careful to keep this fact from the gallery public. Suzannah's life was lived more than ordinarily in separate boxes; the first and primary box was the silent world she inhabited when sculpting. The second was family-sized; her father had been a bus conductor and her mother a school secretary. Suzannah had done well at school, without being brilliant, and it was some surprise, not least to her art teacher, when she won a university place, completed a thesis, and began to sell her sculptures. Academia was the third box; the market was a fourth and the gallery and its customers a fifth. A chunk of money out of each sale paid for one really good dress, coat or shoes, for box five wear. Petite, dark-haired and blue eyed, a combination she owed to her mother's Irish origins, Suzannah looked good in most things, unless she made a really drastic mistake.

Eager to head Tom off before he smashed anything, Suzannah readily engaged in conversation with him, leading him to a corner where bottles of wine awaited the opening. Tom grabbed one of these and it seemed to spring open in his big hands; she found a couple of plastic cups. Tom, she could see, was definitely box five. His shoes, she thought, were hand made; his voice, large like the man, was Eton, or possibly Harrow. Tom proved to be knowledgeable about sculpture and his laudatory remarks about her work were the more acceptable. She found herself accepting a dinner invitation and was glad to leave the gallery and its anxiety behind her for a while.

They ate at a restaurant that Tom might have nicely judged, being just as able to tell background from her voice as she was from his. The venue was Italian, smart, dark, lively. She found he had a bossy attitude towards ordering food and drink but, tired from her day of preparation, was willing to let him go ahead. He told her about himself; merchant banker ('Ah', thought Suzannah, 'right first go') and his unusual name. 'Better get it out of the way first thing,' he said. 'We don't really know where it came from, probably evolved from Christian, but there it was when we are first recorded in the 1300s and the Christmas of the day got his baronetcy.' The meal proceeded pleasantly, Tom took her home in a taxi and correctly did not ask for admittance. She next saw Tom at the gallery opening and he bowed to her, but did not interrupt the business she was genteelly conducting with potential customers and the odd journalist.

After another couple of Tom-directed dinners, Suzannah decided it was her turn, and that she ought to exercise some will-power or she would be swept along, and no doubt ditched when another interest caught Tom's fancy. She had gathered from his conversation that these fancies were wholly absorbing, that he researched whatever subject currently interested him, intelligently and diligently, then filed it away and moved on. She had hit The Contemporary Artist. Suzannah firmly asked him to dinner on her terms, to the local pub where he seemed equally at home as he had been in the smart restaurant. Her small, chaotic flat being near, Suzannah asked Tom home. Inevitably he started to make love to her; because of his bulk and height, there seemed to be Tom everywhere – above, below, beside, under, on top. Suzannah opened magically and effortlessly, like the wine in the gallery, flowed, and found an exquisite sexual release that she had never before known. Tom seemed to think that everything was perfectly normal.

For the next few days, Suzannah thought constantly about Tom. She saw and heard him when he was nowhere near. She found her body melting into an embrace that was purely imaginary. So beset was she by his ever-present image, that it took Suzannah some while to realise that she had not seen the real Tom for several days. Before she had time to develop her sudden panic into pain, Tom telephoned with a proposition. His family home in Kent boasted a separate, and never used, small ballroom, with a pantry and all the usual facilities. This his parents would be glad to loan to Suzannah. She could take her meals with them or cook for herself. She could be as independent as she liked or mix in with the household. Tom would take her down at the weekend for her to decide.

Suzannah liked Tom's parents at once. The father, George, was Tom in body, and the mother, Miranda, Tom in spirit. She had the energy and determination, the concentration. George was vague, a bit weary looking. The ballroom, light, clean and vacant, Suzannah loved. George told her that it was built in the 1880s when the then Lord Christmas had become involved, to his great benefit, in the new business of popular publishing. The ballroom had served until 1916, when the only son, Charles, had been killed on the Somme. George told Suzannah that on some still evenings he fancied he could hear music from the ballroom, an assertion that Miranda roundly denounced as deluded. Suzannah liked to feel that some soft musical presence was watching over the ballroom, a presence undeterred by its use as a hospital during the 1939-45 war and as a barn thereafter.

Having approved her studio, Suzannah returned to town with Tom to pack his car full of her working gear and clothes. They returned to dine with George and Miranda, candlelight and plate and even a butler. She could see that Tom was laughing gently at her, for which she repaid him when he crept into her bedroom, like the young master seducing the servant. In the morning she settled into her studio, ordered what materials she needed, walked into the village to try the shops and the pub, and felt herself blessed. In the following couple of weeks she worked hard and satisfactorily, accompanied Miranda on several morning visits, ate on her own in the week and at the house on weekends. Tom, away on business in New York, neither telephoned nor wrote, but such was Suzannah's content that she hardly noticed. She had to struggle to keep up with Miranda, who had taken her cause to heart and was introducing her to 'useful people'. Miranda had also taken her to the local art gallery/museum and Suzannah had offered to help with the catalogue, or small restoration work.

The whirlwind of Miranda's activity was to finally burst on a dinner party, given in Suzannah's honour, at the end of the week when Tom returned from New York. It would be seen that the Christmases appreciated their new guest and that, despite her voice, she was socially acceptable. Miranda had asked delicately about clothes, and Suzannah had told her of the box five dress policy, which Miranda commended. However, Susannah looked forward more eagerly to seeing Tom – to feeling Tom – than to her party. She was on the look out on the Friday morning when Tom was due. But when Tom's car drew up, the door opened – the wrong door, the passenger door – and out got a lovely, slim, perfect specimen of young womanhood, her shining hair floating in the breeze, her gestures graceful. Tom joined her and she leant into him, laughing. Suzannah could not move because an elephant was crushing her to the ground and her feet were in a bog. As Tom turned round to greet her, and saw her distress, his own face flushed bright red and then crumpled. He appeared to be in the same bog, though without the elephant. He introduced his friend Sophie. Seeing that Sophie was regarding them both with interest, Suzannah drew on childhood lessons of survival, climbed out of the bog, slipped off the elephant and came forward to shake Sophie's hand and smile. Tom and Sophie went on to the house and Suzannah called after them to excuse herself from lunch, pleading work.

Susannah did not put in an appearance at dinner, which George guessed was due to nerves, but which Miranda rightly attributed to Sophie or, tracing the problem to its root, to Tom. Briefly alone with him, she accused Tom of putting his foot in the smooth running of her Suzannah project. Tom hung his head, truly contrite, somewhat bewildered by the mix of his own feelings. Sophie went to bed early to get some beauty sleep, and also to warm up after dining in an inadequately heated room, wearing a thin dress destined to impress Tom and his father. They had both thought she looked a bit wan, mistaking her chilliness for poor spirits, and she received the attention she had aimed for, if for the wrong reasons. Miranda was sharp with Sophie, as she habitually was with the various girlfriends lightly introduced by Tom and as lightly let drop. Miranda could not understand how a reasonably intelligent woman could fail to see that Tom's interest was perfunctory, nor could she fathom why, warned by herself about the likely temperature of the room, Tom's female guests habitually wore the scantiest of clothing. She herself wore bright woollens and long sleeves, her feet shod in warm boots. She also had a hearty appetite and did not leave the sustaining food pushed to one side of her plate.

Wrestling with his own contrition, Tom went to the kitchen and scooped up the sandwiches that had been left for Suzannah, a bottle of burgundy and one of champagne. Suzannah let him into the warm little pantry. Tom set down the sandwiches and silently opened both bottles. He sat on the table and looked at Suzannah. 'My mother says I've put my big feet in it,' he finally said. Suzanah regarded him gravely. 'You've done nothing wrong,' she said, 'we made no commitments.' 'I'm not sure that's true,' Tom replied, 'Explicit promises, no. I-love-yous, no. But we both offered and received something. I was impolite to bring Sophie with me. I was cowardly and stupid not to think about our relationship, what it meant to me. I'm sorry.' Suzannah thought this was a handsome apology and said so. She was also extremely hungry and yearned for the burgundy.

She bit into a sandwich and washed it down, looking at Tom. 'You are, you were, quite free,' she said. 'I don't know if I want to be free,' said Tom. Suzannah ate, sipped, sighed. 'I think I got you mixed up with something out of Mills and Boon,' she said. 'I didn't ask enough, didn't want to know enough about the real you.' She pondered. 'The problem isn't really this Sophie,' she concluded, 'it's that there will always be Sophies. They won't mean anything much to you, but they will to me. I'll become crabby, nasty. It's no good, Tom. We're from different worlds. In all this time it has never occurred to me to get you to meet my mum and dad, yet I've leeched onto yours.' For the first time, Tom was angry. 'You are not a leech,' he said firmly, 'and I am a fool. Sophie and I will return to town in the morning so that nothing happens to spoil your party. You will be wonderful, and I will curse myself for not being there to see you.' He took her in his arms and they hugged and kissed. He walked off back to the house and she watched his figure diminish, darken and disappear. She finished the sandwiches, and took the champagne to bed with her.

In the morning, Suzannah stood under a hot shower to disperse the champagne, drank tea and ate toast, took another, longer, hotter shower for the burgundy, brushed her tongue as well as her teeth. She went to the house to help with last-minute preparations, arranged flowers (at which she was very good) and lunched with Miranda and George, soberly. When it was time, she applied make-up and dressed in her favourite red, swishy dress. Miranda had been doubtful about red, because of Suzannah's blue eyes, but Suzannah had long discovered that while any orange tone was a disaster, crimson reds became her very well. She had brushed back her hair so that its natural curls sprang up around her head, a soft look that emphasised the fine set of her neck. Feeling cold outside in her finery and cold inside, as if she existed outside time, Suzannah went to let the party begin. It was an outstanding success. The guests mixed well, the food was excellent and Suzannah was able to maintain her share in the conversation without difficulty, partly because of the morning visits with Miranda, where she had gleaned the local gossip and picked up an idea of family connections. The better the party went, the more confident Suzannah became, and the more pleased Miranda. George was seen to steal several longing glances towards the quiet morning room, but any escape was forestalled by a quick glance from Miranda, like an optical lasso. When the guests had finally gone, Suzannah and Miranda took a coffee and brandy together. Suzannah stumbled back to her bed and kept Tom firmly where she had put him, away out of her thoughts.

Back to her usual routine in the studio, Suzannah thought it was time to do something to make some money. Her new contacts may be well and good for the future but she needed some present income. It was not too early to think of Christmas goods, and of her market stall, neglected for a few weeks. She decided on some of her Little Men, but in Christmas costume. She made a mould bigger than usual, about three feet high. She retained the floppy hat, her signature on these small, plaster men, but added pom-poms. The body, adjusted to its new size, seemed big. The hands and feet were big. As Suzannah finalized the head, she tweaked the ears, so that they slightly stuck out, seeming to hold up the cap. It suddenly struck her that the mould looked a bit like Tom. When she began to cast from the mould, and then to paint, the resemblance increased. She made ten men and decided that would do, a limited edition. At the end of the week Suzannah said temporary goodbyes and thanks to Miranda and George and went off to reclaim her flat and her market stall.

Suzannah used a local garage as a warehouse for her market stuff. She stored nine of the Men and took the tenth to take orders. Some of the original, smaller Little Men made up a large part of the rest of the stall, with some watercolour postcards and some pen-and-ink sketches. A yell went up of 'Hiya Suzie,' as she set up shop, and there was her favourite fruit-and-veg man, who always looked as if he had just dug potatoes, even when he washed up for the pub, and the leather goods lady, posher than Miranda, and the youngsters on the lampshade stall; the china stall bearing mugs whose transfers had slipped so that the pattern became unintentionally abstract, the Indian sari and scarf stall with its distinctive smell of unbleached cotton. The market was crowded and trade was good. Suzannah took orders for three Christmas Men. She immersed herself in the feel of the market, the sound, the plastic cup of tea that warmed her fingers, the cigarettes she smoked with the veg man. The market was the only place she indulged this vice.

At 6.00pm, tired but elated, she took her stock back to the garage, locked it up, and went to pay her parents a long-overdue visit. Her father, uncritical and eager to see her as always, cried, 'Sue, where have you been?' when he opened the door, smiling and taking her hands, cocooning them in his for warmth. Her mother, more cautious, welcomed Suzannah in with eyebrows just slightly raised. 'It's been a while,' she said, just allowing a hint of a question to be heard. All at once Suzannah, usually reserved, decided on telling them about Tom (the expurgated version), Miranda and George, and the studio. They were both fascinated. 'Our little girl!' exclaimed her father. Her mother wanted to know details of Miranda's tactics, how she had managed the introductions and the party. She wanted to understand the studio, what it meant for Suzannah's work, and whether Suzannah could drop the market stall, which she had always decried. Suzannah told them about the Christmas Men, about the mould, how she had managed the casting. By then her father was getting restless for his television, so Suzannah went out to the shops opposite to get fish and chips for her father, a Chinese take-away for her mother, and a curry for herself. She was used to this round trip – it took a bit of Miranda-style organising; order Chinese first because they took longest; order fish-and-chips second; wait in Indian take-away and pig out on hot gram; collect

Indian, fish-and-chips and finally Chinese, all hot. On her return, they watched television, and ate, and Suzannah's father asked her to stay over, as he always did, and she insisted on going back to her flat, as she always did, and he made his customary call to the local taxi firm that he trusted with his precious prize, and gave her, as usual, her fare money. He waved her off. 'Come soon, Sue, come soon!' but it was Suzannah's mother who stood wistfully by the gate, looking at another life drive off, a life she would never have, having given hers to the suburbs, the husband she loved, and the daughter she had bred to leave them behind.

Suzannah's life settled into an agreeable routine: work in the studio in the week, with a half day at the museum catalogue, return to the flat and market on Saturday and visit her parents, return to Kent on Sunday evening and eat with Miranda and George. Sometimes Tom was there on the Sunday and that was fine, or nearly fine; Suzannah treated him as the son of her patrons. She had started work on something really complicated and absorbing – statuary that would reflect a woodland location, seeming light and insubstantial, capable of moving in wind or rain, and of reflecting sunlight. In these preparatory stages she was mostly concerned with drawing, and with trying different materials. She realised how much her inspiration owed to her setting at the Christmases and walked in the woods, committing to memory the play of light. She read in the library, learning of the family and local history. The library held a painting of the Charles Christmas who died on the Somme. Smart in his dress uniform, he seemed to smile benignly at her. He was very like Tom. Charles was George's uncle; he had died without issue and George's father had inherited, which was probably good for the family fortunes, because he had been an astute businessman. George was blessed with enough of his father's ability to follow where he had led. And of course, he had Miranda.

The Christmas Men that Suzannah made in the evenings, musing on what she had observed and read, sold, and she made another batch of ten. Then one weekday, when drawing a particularly delicate part of her statuary project, Suzannah was surprised by Tom bursting into her studio, carrying a Christmas Man, which he set down on her worktop. Tom looked at Suzannah; he was furious, his eyes mad and the veins in his neck bulging. He tried for speech but it was beyond him. Finally, 'Well?' he said, 'well? What have you got to say? Are you so spiteful?' Suzannah looked from him to the Man and controlled a fit of giggles. 'It wasn't meant,' she said, not pretending to misunderstand. 'It just came out like that. I didn't think anyone would put two-and-two together.' 'Two-and-two!' spluttered Tom. 'Two-and-two! You stand there and talk to me about two-and-two! Do you know these are changing hands at two hundred pounds each?' Suzannah's eyed widened. 'Two hundred pounds!' she said, 'I sold them at twenty-five!' Tom's fury, if possible, grew. 'You sold them! Twenty-five pounds! That's rich. Is it not enough to go through life saddled with the name of Christmas? Do you know, any merchant bank worth the name with whom I trade has one of these in its offices and hides it as I walk in? Can you imagine that? Everywhere you go, go to work, fools fall about laughing?' 'I'm so sorry,' said Suzannah. 'I'm really sorry. It never occurred to me.'

Tom cast himself into a chair, sprawled there, groaned. He looked up at Suzannah and saw the Christmas Man beside her. In spite of himself, his lips began to twitch. 'Okay,' he sighed, 'okay, if it wasn't malicious, I suppose I can get over it about a thousand years from now, before the firm goes bankrupt.' Suzannah had been thinking: 'Wait,' she said, 'don't speak.' She lit one of her Saturday cigarettes. 'Okay,' she said between draws, 'here's what we do. I'm going to cover the mould with resin and give it to you to put in your office. You'll have the mould, you'll know there can be no more copies. And I'll make a bigger one, as if that were the original, decorate if finely, and you can keep it in a display cabinet, have the last laugh. I'll sign it and give you provenance.' Tom looked sceptical for a bit. Then he went to her fridge, got some white wine, scrupulously offered Suzannah a glass and sipped his own. 'It's a deal,' he said. For much of the rest of the week, Tom sat still for Suzannah while she worked feverishly. At last the two Christmas Men were ready, fine and good, the one glowing with auburn resin, the other with gold paint and peacock colours, dressed in materials Suzannah had found in the attic, lace, velvet, delicate shoes. Finally they were ready. Tom and Suzannah were both exhausted, him with sitting still, her with working. She had turned on the radio to help Tom pass the time. As Suzannah threw down her brush, a soft shuffle was playing on Jazz FM; Tom put his arms around her soldiers, massaged her stiff neck, and they slowly began to dance. It was good to feel his arms, good to move freely; the music changed to a rag and they danced on, as if a waltz were playing. Lifting her head from Tom's shoulder, it seemed to Suzannah, just for a second, that the ballroom was full of couples swaying, some tears shed, some laughter, and there in the crowd, distinct against the mist of floating pastel dresses, was Charlie Christmas in his dress uniform, gravely looking at her, questioning. Then Take Five began and the room went back to normal, her sculptures clear again, the chair on which Tom had sat, her brushes. That evening Tom and Suzannah ate with Miranda and George; it was cosy, even the butler familiar now that Suzannah knew him from his village day job of potman in the pub. At one point, Tom and his mother chatting nineteen to the dozen, George looked at Suzannah and hummed a little waltz song, raising his eyebrows. Suzannah nodded, and smiled. 'What is it?' cried Miranda. 'Nothing,' Suzannah replied, 'just something that came from my Irish background.'

Thinking of backgrounds, Suzannah thought it was time Tom met her parents. She tried to describe them to him. 'My father wanted to call me Susan, after his mother,' she said, 'but my mother wouldn't hear of it. She wanted Siobhan, but Dad refused to call me something he couldn't spell. So they settled on Suzannah. Dad always calls me Sue, Suzie, or Suzie Q, or when I was little, Squib. Mum always calls me Suzannah. They are both interested in me, in my art, in my career. Neither likes the market, especially Mum. If she goes for fruit and veg and sees me, she ignores me. Dad met all sorts when he was a bus conductor, all races, lots of languages, coins from different parts of the world, I had quite a collection. When I was little I used to love to punch a ticket, and he had to put the money in. He let me do it, although money was tight. Mum would have loved to be self-sufficient, cooking and sewing, but in fact is a poor cook and a worse seamstress. She was, however, a very good school secretary. Imagine Miranda with a whole school to run, what bliss.'

Tom was intrigued and excited about paddling in this new stream, and offered to accompany Suzannah on her Saturday market – and parents-visit. There was a bit of a sticky moment at the market when the original Little Men came out of their box, however, they served to show Tom that they originated before Suzannah knew he existed. Tom chatted with the other stallholders and he did not break anything, although he came close a couple of times. When they went on to her parents' house it was, as usual, Dad who opened the door. 'I've heard about you from our Sue,' he said, 'come on Suzie, I thought you'd never get here.' Mum was more formal, asked Tom about the market. Suzannah, seeing that this was an attempt to recruit Tom for the anti-market side, headed her off by introducing Tom to the takeaway run. This he found entrancing, and popped into the off-licence to add wine and brown ale to the hoard. 'How did you know to get brown ale?' asked Suzannah; Tom put his finger to the side of his nose and then told her he had asked the licensee. Seeming to agree with both Mum and Dad at once about the choice of television programme, a difficult task as their tastes were diametrically opposed, Tom passed a pleasant evening. He drove Suzannah home; they both paused but Suzannah did not ask him in. She nearly called him back, but the telephone began to ring; Dad, asking if she got home alright – and the moment passed.

Tom had to spend a week in Switzerland, so Suzannah decided to stay in London and pick up the threads, visit the galleries. In the café at the National Gallery she ran into a young man she had known at university and seen a few times since. Derek was from the same area of London as Suzannah and of similar background, Irish ancestry included; he was now a lawyer. Derek claimed that his London accent was an asset in criminal work; the clients trusted it and the judges pitied it; the opposition did not like to be too hard on him in case it upset the jury. Nothing much upset Derek; he knew himself to be blessed with high intelligence and a quick wit. He was fun to be with, and good-looking in a dark-haired, lean-hipped way. He was not tall, but lithe, his movements quick and deft like his mind. Suzannah always enjoyed herself with Derek, who had made it clear early in their relationship that nothing serious was going on.

'So how goes the up-and-coming lawyer? Clients been nicking the national treasures?' Suzannah asked. 'Budding young artist yourself,' he replied. 'Hi Suze, good to see you.' He got himself tea and they chatted. 'I've been hearing about you,' said Derek. 'Apparently there are some little Christmas gnomes changing hands for a thou.' Suzannah gritted her teeth. 'I sold them for twenty-five pounds,' she told him. 'You never had a grasp of economics,' Derek said. 'Do you remember when I was in *Socialist Worker* and I tried to explain Marxism to you?' Suzannah remembered. She had been more interested in the shape of his mouth and nostrils, and the exact colour of his eyes.

The eyes, bright, laughing, suddenly took on an arrested expression. 'Suze,' he said, 'you're the answer to a prayer. God has put you here in the National Gallery. I have a dinner tomorrow in Chambers; some visiting dignitary and we're all to turn out. Actually I came here to see this latest exhibition, so I'd have something to talk about to the wife and daughters. I have no partner for the dinner.' 'You have no partner? But you always had girls coming out of your ears.' 'Tell the truth, Suze, I'm in a bit of a social desert.' Derek looked not hurt by this, but resigned. 'Even with the blokes, you know, down the pub – if I've got a case the next day, I stick to mineral water. It sets me apart. And if I stop off on the way home, I'm dressed wrong, so I have to go home and change, and it seems like putting on costume, so I don't. I don't mean I never go, it's just become an effort. And I don't get on with the Hooray Henrys in the Chambers. I get on best with my clients. There's some old boys in Chambers I like; in truth, I've sort of become Rumpole. And Rumpole always made me cry. And that's the blokes, mind. With the girls it's worse, being girls. And the posh ones, they expect a bit of rough, and I'm not like that.' He wasn't, Suzannah remembered. He was a kind and attentive lover, but not exciting. Suzannah could imagine Sophie, out for a thrill, looking at her nail varnish, lying back and thinking of England. By now the gallery was closing and they moved on to the crypt at St Martin's, for an early supper. The more they talked, the faster, and the more pronounced their accents. Suzannah found herself telling Derek about Tom. 'So where is this paragon?' he asked. 'In Switzerland.' 'You mean you let him go off? Why don't you pin him down?' 'I'm not sure I want to pin. There's the Sophie problem,' Suzannah explained. 'To be fair, I think you'll always have Sophie problems,' Derek agreed, 'but you'll have to learn not to mind. Meanwhile, come to my dinner.'

Suzannah dressed carefully, donning a dark-blue velvet dress and scraping her hair into an antique comb she had found at the Bermondsey market. Derek called for her, immaculate in evening wear. Suzannah thought that his social problems would not be long-lasting. At the reception she found some people from the Miranda dinner, and these having made other introductions, began to feel less of a stranger and less conspicuous. The dinner and the wines were wonderful. Derek, as always, was abstemious, and drove her home, profuse in his thanks. 'I suppose this Tom bloke being in the picture, you're not interested in anything else?' he asked. 'No,' said Suzannah, 'I'm sort of absorbed.' 'Well, ask me to the wedding,' Derek replied, with a cheerful wave.

A few days later, Suzannah was soaking in a rose-scented bath when Tom indeed entered the picture, crashing through the door and yelling what seemed to be 'Again!' Suzannah eyed him in amazement. She not only smelt like, but resembled a pink rosebud, slim shoulders rising from the steam, slim neck, hair swathed in shampooed furls around her head. She spoilt the image: 'Close the bleeding door,' she yelled back, furious at the draught spoiling her soak. Tom kicked the door shut with his heel and began waving his arms, still shouting 'again!'. 'You've done it again,' he said. 'Do you take pleasure in ruining my career? Is your sole object in life to make mine as difficult as possible?' 'What do you mean?' asked Suzannah, wondering if any more Men had turned up, or been stolen, or copied. (In fact, some cheap fairy-light copies had been made and were selling well, but neither Suzannah nor Tom knew of this.) 'You

54

and Judge John Deed, that's what I mean. The up-and-coming radical lawyer. Your boyfriend.'

'Derek?' asked Suzannah. 'Whatever his name is. Taking you about and flaunting it everywhere.' 'I went to his Chambers dinner,' said Suzannah. 'What's wrong with that?' 'Did you think I wouldn't know?' asked Tom, slighting dropping the decibel level. 'My mother was rung by one of her friends to be told that the nice young artist had a nice new boyfriend. I know we've got no commitment.' Then the decibels went up again. 'I suppose he's better in bed than me,' shouted Tom. Suzannah, now equally angry, hissed back: 'Five years ago, when I last slept with him, he was a kind and considerate lover and quite satisfactory, thank you. And he never burst into my bathroom, or blamed me for his own hurt pride. And he never cheated on me when he was sleeping with me.' Tom, who had sat down on the lavatory seat, making it squeak and slew sideways, reared up again. 'That's it. That's it. I knew it. You were Sophie-ing, to get your own back. Well, stick with the Judge; I'm out of here.' 'Fine,' said Suzannah, 'fine. And leave your key, if you had a key and didn't just break the door down.' The door slammed behind Tom, and opened again a chink as the key was thrown through. It fell into the lavatory, Tom having dislodged the seat in his last fury.

Suzannah lay back in the bath and ran more hot water to do some hard thinking. So Tom was jealous. Was that good or bad? Good, in that it indicated deep feeling for her, bad in that it indicated jealousy and fits of irrational anger. Tom had never before used the key to the flat unless she was with him. It had been given for a practical reason, to help with the market arrangements, not as a token of partnership. Or had it, she asked herself. What did she really think about Tom? Was it just sex, or largely just sex? Had she, did she propose a long-term relationship? Had they ever really been a couple? As she got out of the draught-spoilt bath and wrapped herself in lots of comforting towel, the telephone rang. It was her mother. After the usual preliminaries, the actual reason for the call became apparent. Her mother wanted to know the state of play with Tom. 'Wish I knew, Mum,' said Suzannah, 'wish I knew.'

As neither Tom nor Suzannah wanted to be first to contact the other, there was no further opportunity for explanations. Tom, miserable and angry, snapped at his clients, worrying his chief who had got wind of grumblings of economic discontent. 'It's America, Tom,' he explained. 'If the US of A goes arse about face, what chance we? I know we kept out of the sub-prime market, thank the Lord, but this could be big.' Tom was worried not so much for himself, as for his fiercely independent parents. He had put enough aside in the glory days, in several currencies, in various banks, to survive in reasonable comfort in the long run, or even extravagance in the short term. In fact, he need not have worried about George and Miranda who, always frugal, retained half-full the pots of money that George's father had left them. Tom had been not to Eton, as Suzannah suspected, but to the village school and local grammar school before Cambridge. His excellent first-class degree and family connections were good enough introductions to his first post in a merchant bank and indeed, gave him something of an boy-makes-good edge. However, news of a possible impending economic downturn did nothing to soften his temper. Suzannah meanwhile stayed cool, going back to her studio and what had become comfortable weekend meals with Tom's parents. Miranda noted that Suzannah never froze in the dining room but looked good in her jumpers and boots. Suzannah, herself now in easy enough financial circumstances, insisted on paying rent. Without her knowing, George put this aside for her in a specially created savings account, intending to repay her by buying one of her own works when the time was right. When not absorbed in her ethereal project, Suzannah passed the time by applying for a grant, carefully researching the likes and dislikes of the providing agencies. The museum retained her to put on a special exhibition, paying her a small fee.

    Tom and Suzannah spent Christmas with their respective parents. Suzannah's gained rather more profit from this than Tom's, as his acerbity continued to be made felt by grunts and snaps. Suzannah spent an evening at the pub with Derek and filled him in on Tom-events. Derek was rather impressed by the bathroom scene and they debated whether Tom could be accused of trespass. Rather wistfully, Suzannah was forced to give up the idea. Derek himself was making headway with the daughter of his head of Chambers, who had got under his defences due to her gentle eyes and charming deference to his opinions. 'Is her name Hilda?' Suzannah asked. 'Why the hell should she – oh, I get it, Rumpole again. No.' He waited a few seconds and then said: 'Actually, her name is Mathilda.' They both burst into fits of giggles. To celebrate his progress with Mathilda, Derek asked Suzannah to dinner, choosing the Italian restaurant where she and Tom had first dined, thus causing Suzannah to sigh a little until Derek forcibly pointed out to her the difficulty of eating with someone who played rather disgustingly with their food and answered conversational gambits at random. Suzannah apologised and they spent an enjoyable evening thereafter, guessing the occupations of their fellow diners, with more abandon and less accuracy at each course. By the cheese they were quite riotous. Suzannah's mood quickly changed when she got home and found an envelope in Tom's writing. Inside was a note to the effect that, having learnt the Men in his office were now worth upwards of £5,000, he was enclosing a cheque for that amount. Suzannah cut the cheque up into dancing fairy dolls that spelt SLOB, and returned it.

For the following twelve months Tom and Suzannah did not see each other, or rather escaped the regard of the other if their paths crossed. Tom, attempting to achieve some stability in his own sector of what came to be called The Credit Crunch (sounds like a punk band, said his boss), increased his globe-trotting. He had several Sophie-esque flings, but as he remained gloomy and irritable, these did not last, and word got round in his own circle that Tom Christmas was best avoided. He seemed to have personalised the economic doom and gloom when what was needed was some light relief. Suzannah got her grant and her work on the ethereal project benefited as she was able to indulge herself with the materials she used. She had several meals with Derek and, on the eve of his engagement to Mathilda, they slept together. This they both regretted, because each derived therefrom considerable enjoyment. Suzannah was pleased to have male arms around her, pleased to have pleasure, and was sorry that someone so easy to talk to, so civil and yet so sharp, of her own world, was necessarily going out of her life. Derek admitted to himself that his gentle young fiancée lacked Suzannah's salt; but also that, if he had wanted a salty diet on a permanent basis, he would have done something about Suzannah a long time ago. Sitting in his blue-striped boxer shorts at her kitchen table on the morrow, his dark hair fetchingly tangled over his eyes, he questioned Suzannah on the Tom affair. 'There is no affair,' snapped Suzannah. 'Yes there is, you practically live with his parents and you avoid him.' 'Stop the inquisition, I'm not one of your bloody clients.' 'No, thank God. Give me an honest burglar any day rather than a sexy, half-Irish artist suffering from inverted snobbery. And get some clothes on if you don't want to go back to bed.' 'Clothes yourself. And anyway, you can't, not from today, you are now a man spoken for. But Derek, doesn't it bother you, to hitch up with someone out of our world? You were the Marxist.'

'I wasn't a Marxist, I was a Trot. Not that you ever knew the difference. I still am, I haven't changed my opinions. But my opinions, my dear *ignoramus inamorata*, are about the class system, for which I blame the organisation of our society, not individual people who live in it and cannot escape its effects. That is why I don't belong to any party, because I found they all tried to individualise a system, which leads one down a Robespierrian path. I just try to live my life according to my principles. Hence the burglars etc. They are also products of the system, I can attempt to ameliorate its effects on them. By the way, your Tom ('not my Tom') recognises this. It's what merchant bankers do, they study the system and try to make some cracks at some times and heal them up at others, to make the juices of capitalism flow. And even you must have realised that this system now threatens to implode under its own weight, and seen the irony that it's a Labour Party financial genius who has, to mix my metaphors, his finger in the dyke. Sorry, quite a speech.'

'It's okay. Who else can I talk to, who knows me now, and comes from where I come from? It's that as well – it's just more comfortable to be around someone who sounds like me, who knows all the sights and smells of my bit of London, who calls me Suze and is kind to me.'

'Dear Suze, I shall miss you. I do know what you mean, but you don't have to lose your past. You don't have to shut doors in your face, either. Damn, I wanted to take you back to bed, now I daren't, in case I fall in love with you. For Christ sake get dressed, woman.'

So Suzannah and Derek parted in fond friendship. As always when bedevilled by personal problems, Suzannah immersed herself in work. Her creation now filled a large part of her studio. It suggested trees in its slim, polished wooden uprights, ending in fans of split bamboo from which glass drops trembled; the floor was rubber, with rock-like bumps and glass rivers. The whole was powered by electricity so that it was in movement. There were several light, imperfectly formed plastic figures, shapes suggesting rather than defining people and animals, that could be added to or subtracted from the scene by the viewer according to taste, so that the viewer in turn became artist. The viewer could also change the colour of the lighting, creating sun, or twilight, autumn or spring. The change in light affected the movement, which was stilled by bright and increased by greyer tones. One exquisite sculpture was fully formed, a young deer made from shiny wood, whose colours danced as the glass drops shook. It was altogether very fluid, very light, massive only in its size, tempting one to enter its space. George loved it and spent much time sitting on a stool which Suzannah had helped him carve, so that he became part of the sculpture. Suzannah told him firmly that he was now part of the exhibition and would regret it when he was installed with it in the London gallery where it was to be displayed, as part of the grant prize.

Suzannah and her parents spent Christmas with Miranda and George. Her father and George got on very well, being, Suzannah realised, of much the same non-judgemental, caring character. Miranda and her mother were equally compatible, although their relationship was given to short, fierce disputes, which both relished. Suzannah suspected Miranda of thinking up fresh subjects of controversy overnight. Tom was in Venezuela and telephoned, speaking to both fathers, on a day when the three women were sales-shopping in the nearest market-town. George's face, on their return, was alight with pleasure at the call. 'Tom phoned, Tom,' he called out as they were getting out of the car, 'just fancy, our boy, out there, and he phoned.'

Suzannah returned to London to prepare her exhibition. Her parents stayed on with George and Miranda, seemingly set on underlining Derek's theory that people overrode class. Suzannah spent most of her time in the gallery. She nipped and tucked, tried different lighting. The champagne came and the first night invitations. Derek and Mathilda were to be guests of honour. Suzannah had met and liked the shy young woman, and found her adoration of Derek touching. She had never adored anyone like that, certainly not Tom. On the eve of the opening, Suzannah was playing with complete darkness for the surround of the exhibit and green light within. She was therefore unaware of the arrival of a large person until Tom tripped over a cable. 'For fuck's sake don't move,' she yelled, as Tom, trying to steady himself, dislodged a tree shape she had spent an hour getting into position. Tom froze, immobilised as much by the beauty that surrounded him as the beauty who shouted at him. Suzannah regarded him gravely, and then changed the lighting to violet, and then soft red. Tom felt his hurt assuaged as he looked and wondered. Sitting back on her heels, Suzannah looked at the spectacle: first, she saw that the tree was better in its new position; second, that big, solid Tom did not spoil her airy sculpture. Rather, he fulfilled it. Suzannah realised that she had made him a setting, that she had worked all this time on framing a void. That, of course, was why George had looked so right sat in its centre. She came slowly towards Tom, who opened wide his arms. She entered his embrace, returning it, holding as much of him as she could. They began to dance, turning, waltzing. Both were crying. As Suzannah's eyes began to clear she saw one of the red-lit plastic figures raise his cap, as Charlie Christmas said goodbye.

Love and Lives

Circumstances

I was once told:

'In the circumstances,
within the context
of the situation,
I love you.'

The Sylph and the Stag

She was to be a sylph. Maybe she was a little on the heavy side, and a bit too old to be a realistic sylph but, as common in choral societies, most people were a bit old to be most things, unless they were a bit young. She was to wear a flowing shift, of which she was fond, because it undoubtedly helped the illusion of fragility. He was a deer, which suited him, because he was timid, wary, fugitive, but with a sleek beauty. The choral society was to perform a modern oratorio with costume and some minimal staging. After months of weekly rehearsals all were to meet for a rehearsal weekend at a country hotel: the sopranos, who found the top notes difficult; the basses, who had problems with the rhythm; the tenors who were good individually but had trouble singing in unison; and the altos, who sang melodiously but too quietly. Now the principals would be chosen and parts perfected.

They had been friends, the sylph and the deer, throughout the rehearsals, sometimes sharing a car to and fro. They were comfortable together, laughed together and their conversation was wide-ranging. There was, however, an unexplored edge to the sunny fields of their relationship, a dark and obscure forest area in which flourished unbidden the tangled undergrowth of the might-have-been. She was married; he was single, hurt from a divorce. Sometimes when she knocked for him the house would be dark and he would not answer. She would tiptoe away, respectful of his privacy. He had a motorbike and on those days when, riding it, he faced the outside world with bravado he seemed and looked a different being – more stag than deer.

At the weekend's first rehearsal they looked each other out and talked as usual. He had ridden his motorbike, she had driven her car. She had paid extra for a single room, for privacy. Somehow, whether because of the wine they drank at dinner, the fact he remained motorbike-garbed most of the day, or because it was time, they ended up together in her bed. When she had, very occasionally, allowed herself to begin to picture such a foray into the forest of passion, she had been stayed by consideration of her appearance; of the chicken-skin and bat-wing areas of her flesh and of her face without make-up. To her relief, while he did not appear to notice these deficiencies, she saw that his skin also, in places, resembled chicken or bat.

Thus, she being reassured and he unobservant, their coupling was friendly; rather than wild and scary; it was natural and satisfying. She felt no guilt. They both, however, gained a dimension, a warmth, a colour. The need they felt to escape suspicion (a futile endeavour, since they had been the subject of gossip for months) lent an extra excitement to their lovemaking. Subsequently, at the lunch break and every opportunity thereafter, the deed lived up to the imagination, until their mutual passion overflowed, bringing magic to the external world. Once, he left briefly to bring in vegetables from his allotment for the collective supper. She leant, ecstatic, over his supplies, the things he had planted and tended, fingering the earthy new potatoes, the shiny red onions with their silver bloom, the carrots with their fronds of green.
    The self-bestowed benediction that illuminated them resulted in their being named principals. She was to be the alto Sylph, an intended sacrifice to the lust of his bass Stag. The tenor Huntsman would finally hold him at bay while the soprano Goddess of the woods would assist her last minute, half-regretful flight. He worried about this outcome, seeing in it a prediction of their final parting. The weekend over, however, their lovers' meetings continued, as best they could; they did not suffer from protracted separations because, as principals, they were called for extra rehearsals.
    Finally came the performance week. In costume, he looked magnificent, naturally bronzed, with deerskin on his shoulders and a high headdress. She looked delicious, she shimmered in her shift of forest greens and pastel blue, soft pleats falling from a high yoke, her hair carefully disarranged. Both had lost weight and gained muscle-tone due to their unaccustomed exercise. For the first four nights of their performance they played and sang beyond themselves, singing the forest edge, the living undergrowth of passion. They transformed for their audience the shabby church hall into a place of magic, splendour and danger. On the final night, when the Huntsman held him at bay and the Goddess drew the Sylph stumbling away, weeping, the Stag let out a great and unwritten howl. The composer found it so good, he added it to the score, but it was never repeated, in later performances, with such pathos.

The Brown Cardigan

We know the love affair is going badly when the brown cardigan appears. Actually there are two varieties of brown cardigan; one is short at the back, a mere fringe covering the shoulders, with long side panels; the other is long all over. In either case they are worn hugged round the thin body, elbows out, back bowed, hair uncombed. When the love affair is going well, she wears white, or gay black and white check, even the occasional pink. The hair is fetchingly arranged, the make up done, the smile wide. The love affair is not one love affair, but a series of one-two-several night stands with different men. It would be unfair to presume these were all sexual encounters; they are romantic. The men are cut from the same mould; tall, indefinite, a bit glazed.

A serial attempt at finding a partner is not really any different from a persistent effort with one man, in which both sides of the couple adjust their presenting personality, their looks, their tastes. And people, any one person, will constantly change. Over the day, at work, home, shopping, they wear their different personalities as they change their clothes. They fit themselves into each new scene. They adjust their interactions with each set of different others. One's voice changes according to situation and location – accent, speed of delivery, phraseology; language. Seeking to be understood, to register emotion, to complain, to express joy. Nothing lasts longer than the moment it is. The moments add up differently for each side of the couple; one partner may multiply perceived adjustments, the other may divide them. A full score (any number beyond toleration) may be counted by one partner, so that they stand on the brink of rupture, while to the other the same score is unimportant. Over the months, years, according to situation and routine, one projected personality may crystallise – tendonitis of the personality, bad; a second may disintegrate – insanity, worse. And because of these daily/monthly/annual adjustments, there are brown cardigan secrets, white-cardigan lies. Although these secrets and lies may be corroding, outing them is seldom of use to anybody, they are adjustable parts of the normal camouflage. 'Truth is a bourgeois reality'. I quote, but that's a different story.

So, little brown bird, don't fall off your perch when it no longer holds you comfortably, when it is insecure, too sharp, prickly, or when another one seems a better bet. Steady yourself, raise your white wings and pin on your smile. Throw away both brown cardigans. Get your hair done. You are no different to any of us, except in your willingness to put the past behind and try again.

The Moustache

There was a train from their small town to the city. It was a dismal affair, grimy, grimly festooned with graffiti, and smelling as if several wet dogs had been left overnight to dry off in the carriages. The passengers were a collection of misfits: the obese, those swilling in beer and unsteady on their legs, an occasional couple who liked courting in public, mothers not afraid to change their babies' nappies, and young women on shopping trips who had starved to fit into the size sixes. These young women had make-up so perfect it was like a plastic film, hair so lavishly cut and coloured that it seemed painted and crafted onto their heads. If Louise travelled alone, she sat with her back to the guard's compartment, to have at least the illusion that help was near to hand. He was behind her even though, no doubt intimidated, he rarely put in an appearance. To add to the gloom, the train went underground for the last few miles, like a grub burrowing.

Exiting the city station one Saturday in company with her husband, Louise followed him into his favourite pub, which retained its old-fashioned mahogany counter with brass rail well-polished, its scarred, round wooden tables set in alcoves. A plastic-filmed woman came up and addressed Sean, who affected not to know the intruder, flushing scarlet and tugging at the hairs of his scanty moustache. Louise thought perhaps he had grown the moustache so that he could pull it, for comfort, rubbing his stubby fingers against the hairs that framed his lips. Otherwise he was a smart man, who cared for his clothes and his hygiene. His expansive shoulders and general sturdiness betrayed his farming origins, but as yet his embonpoint was in its very early stages. A certain glazed and wary look about Sean prevented Louise from asking what the woman had wanted. They carried on as if there had been no interruption. That was their way. Louise disliked fuss and bother: she felt secure in her marriage and protected in Sean's presence, the availability of his broad shoulder, just above her head. Sean was shy of discussing his feelings. It was, after all, not uncommon to be accosted in the city's pubs by a stranger with something to sell, tee-shirts, trainers, socks or other more exotic ware. Indeed, the legend that one could thus buy an elephant was celebrated by an elephant statue in the market square.

Some time later, Louise had a few days' leave. She travelled alone to the city, spotted the woman who had spoken to Sean with a group of friends, arm-in-arm, laughing. Louise was pointed out and, she felt, crowed over.

'Scallys,' thought Louise, 'what could he want with her?' Disturbed nevertheless, Louise sought sanctuary in Sean's pub – it had the nearest decent Ladies' room to the station. The woman came up and sat at her table. She looked chic, with a scarf wound round her rather long neck. Louise was reminded of one of the songs Sean sometimes delivered in his Irish grandfather's accent:

> *Her eyes they sparkled like diamonds*
> *her neck it was just like a swan's*
> *her hair it hung over her shoulder*
> *tied up in a black velvet band.*

The woman's hair was black, long, swinging. Sean had always liked black hair and Louise's was an indeterminate blonde.

'I'm a friend of your Sean,' said the woman. 'I don't know if he talks about me. We go back a long time.' The diamond eyes shone strongly. Louise did not reply, sat very still. 'Only I don't want to get him into trouble,' said the woman, 'but he got me these tickets...'

Louise felt her stomach tug and wobble. Sean had told her how some of his mates profited from the tickets they were allocated, either reselling them, which was illegal, or giving them away for services rendered, ditto. He had pulled his moustache as he told her, and Louise had wondered if this was tantamount to a confession. She had carefully replied that, in such cases, one must be very sure of the discretion and loyalty of the person to whom the tickets were bestowed.

'...only I did hear,' continued the woman, 'that they didn't ought to. Give away the tickets, like. I thought, when he gave them to me, they might be dodgy, because he kept fiddling with his moustache. You know, rubbing his hand across it, hiding his mouth. Pity, because it's a nice mouth. So I kept the stubs. What I wondered was, like, whether anyone would be interested in buying the stubs.' Louise still made no reply. 'Anyway,' concluded the woman, I'll be here tomorrow, same time. I'll bring the stubs.'

At home that night, Louise watched Sean to see if he matched her image of him. But the image had been built and adjusted over such a long period that it had weathered, was set and resisted inspection. His voice also had been long fitted to her ear; he did not swear or shout, knowing she disliked noise. They had their own language for their own chatter. They rarely had a conversation. Sean said he was going out for an hour and she encouraged him as usual, glad for him to have some male company and to drink his beer, outside the house. However, it was his absence that made her concentrate on her enquiry into her husband. Was he happy with her? Was she too quiet, too prim? What was he like, when standing at the bar, or playing billiards? Were his sleeves rolled up, was his tie in his pocket? It was surely a noisier version of Sean who marked his cue with a flourish, stood his round, occasionally sang his Irish songs:

> *An old man came courting me, hey ding dorum dell*
> *An old man came courting me, me being young*
> *When we went to bed, he lay like he was dead*
> *Maid when you're young never wed an old man*

The smells of the pub, the beer, someone's perfume, a wet jacket, men sweating were all eliminated from Louise's home. She thought of searching through his clothes, looking through his desk, but she was scared of what she might find and shrank from the grubby sneaking. So Louise opted for a bath and an EmmyLou Harris disc.

She thought of how she had once emptied Sean's pockets for the wash and found a bloodied handkerchief. Sean had said 'nosebleed,' had taken it from her and dropped it in the bin. Sean was back before she left the warmth of the bath, called up the stairs, said it was good to be home. He had brought pizzas. Louise usually refused fast food of any type, thought it fattening, disliked the messy waste of the packaging, and if she ate a pizza in a restaurant it was with a side salad. Tonight, however, she ate avidly of her share, surprised at her hunger.

The next day Louise drove herself to the city. It was a boring and in places, dangerous drive, which she usually avoided, but she wanted to be sure of her escape route. Seated in the pub, Louise watched the woman arrive, flashing looks at her friends who stayed by the bar, swinging her hoop earrings, stretching her swan neck, still enveloped in a scarf. 'I've got the stubs,' she said, laying them on the table. She named her price. Then she unwound her scarf, revealing long, thin lines of bruises, black at the edges. 'The price includes damages,' she said. 'Likes a bit of rough, our Sean.'

As Louise considered the bruises and her image of Sean, brought them both into vision on one screen, as if responding to the 'arrange all windows' command for multiple word documents, her fears were dissipated. She replied: 'you are mistaken. I suggest you go to the police.' She left, drove home. Sean had come home early, thought they might do something with her bit of holiday. She watched his hands stroke his moustache with his short, broad fingers; he was gentle, and essentially timid. 'Let's get dressed up and go for a meal,' he suggested. 'One thing – I thought I might shave off my moustache.'

'No, don't do that,' said Louise, 'keep it, it suits you, its part of your personality.'

The Cigarette

The shabby boarding house made no pretence to a sea-view. Instead, it offered post-war utility furniture, sad-coloured, horsehair-filled armchairs, and poorly-framed pictures literally cut from ancient chocolate boxes, mouldering on the flock wallpaper. It was tolerated by a surprisingly faithful clientele because the food was reasonable and prices moderate. That it paid its way was largely due to the proprietress's exploitation of her twins, Sheila and Colin. Now in their twenty-fourth year, they had dark red hair and freckles marking the sort of skin that sizzles in summer sun. They each wore their hair long and it was their main glory, both being tall and thin, and in Sheila's case, having a bust line that owed nothing to silicone but much to her robust mother. Singly, they were well enough but not remarkable, but when they strolled out together and had both taken care of their appearance, the effect was stunning. It was a bit like being faced by the young woman with the high-heeled red shoes in the advertisement for hair dye, who walks head and shoulders above the crowd – but double.

They worked long hours for low pay but remained cheerful, Colin because it was his nature, and Sheila because Colin was content. Their father, a musician, had fled when he entered the labour ward recovery room to find he had inadvertently sired not one, but two responsibilities. Sheila had inherited his musicianship; Colin, his fecklessness. Their mother was loud and confident and frankly vulgar in her satin-bloused decolletée. She had not much regretted the departure of a husband who was more inclined to borrow money from her purse than to earn their keep, and his place was taken by a succession of gentlemen friends with whom Sheila and Colin generally had good relations, being able to jointly stare down any attempt at over-familiarity.

When they took their morning break, after the breakfast-providing and room-cleaning rounds, Colin might suggest to Sheila that they took the evening train to London, not a long journey from their South Coast resort, and enjoy an evening in town. This was a favourite indulgence, although seldom pursued in the season. Sheila loved everything about the trip, from the journey in the old and smelly train, to the arrival at Charing Cross, through the promenade past the theatres to Leicester Square to a Soho restaurant and nightclub, and the return by the morning mail train. She planned what she would wear, down to the last detail.

On this occasion though, at the post-lunch break, Colin said why go all the way to London when their friends were on the spot and the season in full swing. Sheila was disappointed, but not surprised. Colin disliked effort and the thought of perhaps having to iron a shirt, to shower and change and even shave, was enough to deter him from this particular purpose. Nor was Sheila much astonished when Colin failed to fulfil his arrangement of collecting her from the studio flat they shared. (They had long ago agreed that living with Mum and the current gf was not to be endured.) She picked up her bag and went out for the evening, sure to run across Colin at one of their usual haunts.

It was when she could not find that her cigarettes that Sheila became annoyed. She restricted herself to a packet a week, but those few cigarettes she enjoyed, making them last, feeling spoiled, relaxed, in charge. Life might have gone on as usual had not Sheila, midway through bedroom 3 the next morning, spied Colin in the yard with her cigarette packet in his waistcoat pocket. He was bending over the pretty, North Country occupant of bedroom 5 suggesting, Sheila had no doubt, that they took the evening train to London. As he bent forward, tossing back his hair, his waistcoat pocket jutted out, clearly showing its contents. Sheila was sure that it was her cigarette packet, because Colin never bought his own, and their chain-smoking mother used another brand. That he should steal her cigarettes seemed to Sheila the ultimate betrayal. She would have given him the packet, but for him to take it from her bag was villainous, stupid, lazy behaviour.

Sheila recognised, for the first time, that she had no space of her own; the flat she shared with Colin, the boarding house was her mother's, she had no room, not a single cupboard or drawer that was hers and hers alone. She felt miserable, unbalanced as much by her own reaction as by the petty crime.

Feeling the need for action, Sheila downed tools and went to take the coast-road bus, just due to pass their street. The bus crawled along and Sheila dozed in the sun, until she saw that they were about to pass the Hôtel Splendide. Jumping up and ringing the bell, she alighted by the imposing gates. 'Why not,' she thought, 'give them a good lesson.' The Splendide had been advertising for staff for some weeks. The economic downturn had made people wary of booking holidays abroad and the Spendide, with its elegance and comfort, five-star service, jacuzzi and swimming pool, was profiting. Sheila asked to see the manager and, with her experience of the trade, was snapped up. She started immediately, donning the black shirt and white apron provided, to serve at lunch. The tips made her widen her eyes along with her horizons. She called Colin on his mobile, asking him to bring a selection of clothes and her P45.

Sheila soon settled into her new routine, less rigorous and better paid than her Mother's. She borrowed some jeans and was given some T-shirts with the hôtel logo. Long experience of the gfs made her adept at dealing with the manager's half-hearted advances. On her free afternoons, Sheila went to an isolated cove and, not having a swimsuit and enjoying the freedom, swam and sun-bathed naked. It was there Colin found her when he finally turned up with clothes and P45. She was up to her breast in cold, South Coast seawater; her skin was biscuit-coloured, her freckles bleached by the light gleaming on the water, the wet ends of her hair black. Colin knew her body as well as his own; it had been with him all his life; he often sat and talked to her and scrubbed her back when she took her bath. Now, however, he could not bear the beauty of the picture she created and, as she came running out of the sea to meet him, averted his eyes. Sheila wrapped herself in a hôtel towel and demanded news. He had agreed to do both their jobs for two-thirds of their joint wages and could not understand why Sheila sighed at this arrangement. However, having always thought herself indispensable to the smooth running of the business, Sheila was taken aback to find how little she was missed.

A band, whose members Sheila and Colin knew slightly, had been booked to play for a few nights at the Splendide. Sheila, still unsettled, perhaps slightly deranged, by the sudden change in her life, decided to move up a notch. Quite coolly, she selected the youngest member of the group, a comely bass-player, and set out to seduce him. She was successful. Her choice had been informed by past experience of manipulative men who picked a row and then turned up just as she was going to work, expecting her to relinquish her purpose and make up, make love, submit. What with being a twin, and the survivor of a dominating mother and brother, Sheila had decided that she needed to be in charge of future relationships. The bass-player was vague but docile. The relationship prospered. Sheila wondered whether she was more like her mother than she had thought. Inspired by her new-found confidence, Sheila offered to stand in when the singer wanted a free night. At this also she succeeded. The charge between her and the bass-player electrified the performance.

And so began Sheila's career. It was much assisted at the start by her mother, who came to dine at the hôtel after Sheila's first performance to give shrewd advice. The new gf who accompanied her seemed to be a cut above the usual, quiet and reserved, well-dressed. Mother wore a cashmere jumper, encasing her ample bosom. Her short skirt was out of view below the table. 'There's more of your father in you than I thought,' she said, 'and more of me.' She advised Sheila to cut her hair à la Annie Lennox, to ditch the jeans and go for leather and to show off the inherited bosom. She gave Sheila money, to be spent on a re-look. She also had some valuable advice about living with a musician, not least the absolute necessity of having one's own bank account and keeping a healthy balance therein. Sheila started to remember things from her childhood that she had long forgotten; the cuddles, the companionship. Her mother had never differentiated between her twins, never put Sheila down because she was second-born, or because she was a girl. Sheila realised anew how brave her mother had been, bringing up twins alone, when single parenthood was less socially acceptable than nowadays. She followed her mother's advice.

Sheila soon ditched the band and went solo. She retained the bass-player, who proved a considerate room-mate. Colin moved a girlfriend into the studio flat, and their Mother took her on, although she did not raise the joint wages. To save money, Colin and his girlfriend moved into the boarding house. The girlfriend was tolerant of the gfs. When Sheila entered a reality TV talent show, Colin, his girlfriend Mother and gf, could be seen in the audience with their banner, on which they had written 'Go, Sheila, Go.' They did not notice the irony. In fact, Sheila went a long way in the show, although it was, of course, won by a Diana Ross lookalike. Sheila's career profited from the publicity and her repertoire increased. Whether she and the bass player stayed together, is another kettle of fish.

The Dream

Meader came out of the shadow of the trees and hesitated before sitting next to the boy. *Well, well,* he thought, *a chance encounter. My first. I must behave.* Meader was neither short not tall. He was lean, resting lightly on the park bench. His dark hair, now greying, was cropped short, as if his head was covered in iron filings. It was his presentation that made Meader remarkable. He was exceptionally well turned-out; his corduroy trousers were of a bright blue, the colour of his eyes; he pinched the creases so that they stayed centre-knee. Above the trousers he wore a jersey of blue – exactly matching – with sea-green and dusky rose stripes. Sea-green was his favourite colour.

At first Meader said nothing, waiting for the boy to give him an opening. The boy was the antithesis of Meader. His lank, unruly hair fell over a dirty brow. His clothes were cheap and badly creased; sweat shirt, jeans and trainers, all of which would have benefited from washing. What most seemed to worry the boy was his hand, which had been cut in his fall from the bicycle that now lay at his feet, the wheels still turning. Blood flowed from his palm onto his jeans, and smeared his sweatshirt.

'I can ride the bike,' he said. 'There was a stone...'

'I know,' said Meader, 'would you like me to bandage your hand?'

The boy sniffed, unsure. 'OK,' he finally said.

Meader took out a fresh lawn handkerchief, with his initials on it, *ME*. He bound it carefully around the boy's palm, tutting at the jagged edge of the wound. 'I'm afraid you need stitches,' he said.

'I'm not going to no 'osy,' said the boy.

'I know,' Meader replied, 'but you'll regret it later.'

'My Ma'll kill me,' said the boy.

'No, it's alright,' said Meader, 'we'll set the handlebars straight and she'll never know you fell.'

'I didn't fall,' shouted the boy, 'I told youse, there was a stone, a big 'un.'

'It doesn't matter,' said Meader. He reached out for the bicycle, and with some effort, straightened the handlebars. Then he carefully checked the chain, the gears and the brakes.

'What are you doing, here alone?' he asked the boy.

'They didn't want me round 'em,' the boy replied. 'They've all got Nikes, and I haven't.' This was painfully obvious. His trainers were not only scruffy, which would have been acceptable, but of a cheap make, not even pretend Nikes. 'I don't want to hang around them anyway,' said the boy. 'Scallys, all of 'em. And them tarts after them, I don't go for all that slobbering.'

'I know,' said Meader.

'And they laugh at my name.'

'Ivo is a good name,' said Meader, 'later you will be proud of it.'

'How do you know my name? What are you, a poof?'

Whoops, thought Meader. 'Your name is on your bicycle,' he said calmy. It was, but very scratched and hardly distinguishable.

Ivo, however, was satisfied. The blood had stopped running, and he made to take off the handkerchief.

'No, no, keep it on,' said Meader, 'otherwise it will begin again. You really ought to go to the hospital.'

'Old cow at home won't think so,' said Ivo, 'more likely to send me for a carry out.'

Meader knew this was true, and anyway, he had no right to interfere. He did not know how long he would be able to stay, so he determined to give some advice.

'Listen, Ivo. You may not remember what I say, but if you do, it will help you. For a start, you can begin to take care of your appearance. Try the charity shops. You'll be surprised at what you can find. Don't look for Nikes. Soon they'll all have swapped for Adidas, and you can beat them to it. And if you get a decent belt, you can make the jeans your brother will soon grow out of look quite good. Use the iron; in fact, offer to do the ironing for a small reward. Your mother will start to appreciate you more. You will have plenty of girls if you want them, but you may find you are not interested. That's all right. You won't be the only one of your gang going to the gay clubs in Manchester, and if you go first, and can get them in the door, because the bouncers know you, you will start to win acceptance, on your own terms – but that's for later.'

'Thought you was a poof,' said Ivo, but without anger.

'As you grow up, you will find that no trouble,' said Meader, 'in fact, many girls find it good to have a boy who is a friend, without being a boy friend.

'Me Dad'll go spare,' grinned the boy.

'I'm afraid he won't be around,' replied Meader.

Ivo did not seem unduly upset. 'He's a waster anyway,' he said.

'That's probably enough advice,' said Meader, 'except one thing: beware of Uncle George.'

'I know all about him,' said Ivo, scowling, 'I told him, if he tried it on I'd kick him in the cobblers.'

'That's the style,' said Meader. 'Ever seen *Priscilla, Queen of the Desert*?'

'One of them old films comes on Christmas?' asked Ivo. 'I think me Mum watched it, for the costumes.'

'Well, there is a character played by Terence Stamp. Queer as Dick's hatband...' ('never heard that one before,' interrupted Ivo). '...Showing my age,' said Meader, who in fact could have been any age between forty and sixty. 'Well, Terence Stamp tells his young friend how he learnt to fight, and he sees off the baddies. You will also learn to fight. Get those bouncers at the club to show you. There's a nice one, very good looking.' He sighed, 'time to go,' he said, and held out his hand. When he took it, Ivo saw that there was an ugly scar in the palm. He was less impressed by this than by the fact of an adult treating him courteously and wanting to shake his hand.

In bed that night, Ivo nursed his hand, which hurt dreadfully and burned. The handkerchief, still tied round it, was sticky. However, under the bed was a pair of Adidas trainers, nearly new, a bit big, with a sea-green flash. He had bought them from a charity shop with the money he had cheated his mother out of, when she had sent him for fish and chips. Feverish, half asleep, Ivo thought over the day; the strangeness of his encounter occurred to him. 'P'raps I dreamt it,' he thought, 'didn't 'alf give me head a bang.'

Whoopsie

He had a degenerative disease that had recently resulted in double incontinence. Before dealing with the effects of what she called a 'whoopsie', she had absolute need of a cigarette; he hated the wait, in the stench and mud of his involuntary deed. A classic case of sympathy for both sides of an argument. She had not been the dominant partner and suffered still, occasionally, from the overdose of valium that a careless doctor, presented with a frail and nervous woman, had prescribed. But the call to be a carer is indiscriminate and unavoidable. It struck, at the same time it withdrew her male support. Just a few years ago her husband had been upright, strong, going far in his career. Even now, in rare periods of respite care, away from her, with others dealing with the same illness, he regained his previous self to an extent, active, fighting the disease and active in promoting its understanding. But at home, she must face all tasks, whatever their traditional designation. She mended fuses, ironed, drove, gardened, carried heavy loads, wrote letters, balanced accounts, arranged loans (the carer call empties the bank), washed and shaved him, and dealt with the whoopsies. He called and called – why the cigarette, why not after, why his wait? But she needed the time, less than ten minutes, to be away in her head, to be her, not a carer, not an anything to anybody else, to be a smoker of a cigarette, for her alone, because she wanted it so.

Did she not have friends and relations? Like Rabbit, in fact she had many. But the friends, and even more the relatives, found it difficult to cope with the change in their two personalities, his and hers, and in their couple. Relations, but seldom friends, visited; the wheelchair itself and the priority given throughout the house to wheelchair use, upset them. And then, his relations felt she was in some way to blame; if she had not first been ill, if she had not succumbed to valium, might she not have seen portents, such as this and that they had remarked? And if so, with earlier treatment... Did she do enough for him, wasn't she rather rough with him? She could have cut his hair better, and really, those pyjamas did not fit. Was she perhaps waiting for the end, she would do all right then? In her relations' eyes he was too demanding, had always wanted his own way, else she would never have been driven to that doctor. He was a bit of a bully, he was making her old before her time, and his folks never helped, they had the money, they could do more.

In all, it was a relief when the relations went. They came less often as the illness progressed, frightened of being asked to provide even a coupe of hours respite care for a shopping trip. And what would they have done with a whoopsie? Called an ambulance? In such thoughts she wasted her cigarette time and rose to help him. He smiled so sweetly in welcome that it nearly broke her heart.

Weather Report

Cloudless Day

It is cloudless and there is a slight breeze. The sky is perfect Limoges-china blue, paling slightly at the tree line. Impossible to represent that cloudless sky in watercolour, unless one has a hand far steadier than mine. Bo Diddley the cat – le chat jaune – has joined me on my mat and is cleaning industriously, inviting me to help by licking my fingers. Birds chatter and call against a constant hum of machinery, possibly a tractor, clearing the ground of the field beyond. The trees, however, form a green wall, fronted by my bushes and plants. We are enclosed, Bo and I, safe in our garden.
The product of much labour, the garden has profited from a rainy June and is now a place of repose. I showed it to Bo in my arms, when he was tiny, arriving at eight weeks old, abandoned by his mother. He had a room to himself, too small to share the everyday tumble of Odinne, a dog of little wisdom but much activity, arrived

on the same day at the same age. I shared some of Bo's captivity and took him to the garden to smell and hear and see what would become his territory. Now he has claimed it, battling feral cats, moles, snakes, mice, birds. He has tamed the neighbours. Odinne has her park at one end of the garden where she has worn her own pathway. At night, when the traffic stops, she runs free. On this day, 14 July, national day, there are no cars. The roads are as still as the sky, but in the foreground the breeze sends everything moving, a tremblement of dark-cherry leaves, of big yellow flower heads on stick-and-frond bodies. Dark wine lilies rise and fall, deep pink roses with copper and emerald-leafed stems wave royally. The grass itself quivers. Bo's leg is stretched over mine and he sleeps. Content.

Rain

Everything is swinging in the rain, thin, fine rain. Odinne the dog lies under the open barn. She is in season, and sulky. She yearns. The buddleia pokes white noses out into the cold drizzle. Others of its noses browned and I have cut them back, so that it is tall and skinny. The hazelnut branches swing violently, always alive to the least breeze and now chaotic in the wet wind. They creak and menace the roof. The birds in the branches call, cry, high quacks of fear. The bushes are light green in the afternoon light, pale fronds nodding. The light is electric, spotlighting each leaf distinctly.

Is this July, when there were canicules, heat waves, when one could not move for a wall of heat? What is this grainy, spotty, dripping outlook, what is this movement, crepuscular, of branch and leaf? The barn is less substantial in the moist movement, its roof floats, darkened. The stones retain their heat, the walls hold humidity, but the fine, chilling drops make a sharp spatter.

Rose petals fall, their pink has whitened. Yellow plants predominate, autumn colours in summer. The red geraniums provide a shrill note, defiant, summer plants, plants of dryness, canicule survivors, now waving red flags against the grey.

Disturbed, I think of a dog we once had, before Odinne. She was a beautiful, black spaniel; la chienne du village, she danced free, made visits, received tit-bits graciously. She was killed on the road and lies buried in the garden. Because of her, Odinne is on a lead. She warns me of the approach of the postman, driving through a mist of rain, his yellow van an acid flash of colour. He stops, although there are no letters for me. He is distraught. He spotted the first of the village geese, but not the second. He comes in for coffee and a cigarette. We commiserate over death of dog and goose. It stops raining. Time for a walk.

Clouds

They say the life of a cloud is ten minutes maximum. This seems hard to believe, especially of those warrior clouds that glower down on us, growing and gathering force, calling up their reserves, darkening the sky, mustering their armaments of rain. Equally, their pacific cousins, the merry clouds that smile at us, sky ballerinas in tutus, promising not to hide the sun, seem set to dance all day. It is true, however, that neither the warriors nor the ballerinas can be relied upon, as many a clothesline of wet garments and many a dry garden demonstrate. It is easier to believe those clouds will not last which steam and rant and thrust their way, swooping and rolling across the sky, renewed time and again, as if thrown from a celestial hand. Clouds are by their nature inconstant, fickle companions, beckoning us out when we should have stayed in, hissing that we should take cover so that we miss a swim on what turns out to be a beautiful afternoon.

So it is with life. The dark cloud of our own devising which envelops us when we rise gloomily, glowering in our turn at the thought of a whole mood-black day to survive, is dissipated by a chance, kind remark, the trick of a pet. Once Odinne came into the house, collected her basket in her teeth and set it in a patch of sun, curling up proudly, stretching out, riding her basket like a boat, starboard down, port-side up, prow up, stern down. Similarly our good moods are shattered by drops of bad news, spatters of irritations, bureaucratic inanities, the idiot on the radio. Our steaming and ranting moods do not last; we let out the rain of our anger and settle back, refreshed, until the next cloudburst.

We are a cloudy people, grown in a northern garden, sure of rain. We expect our skies to change. We do not make our roots too deep. We have several layers of protective leaves behind which we dwell in secrecy and privacy, letting our blossoms show only occasionally, fearing adverse criticism, relating to each other with reticence; not, in my mother's words, 'getting too thick.' This expression means getting close to someone in haste, throwing away the umbrella of your privacy, taking off your dark glasses so that you are dazzled by someone else's light. Never be dazzled. Always expect the rain.

And yet there is a time in the evening when, whatever the day's weather has been, the light is perfect, just for a short spell between the ten-minute clouds. In this light every leaf on the tree, every branch is clearly visible in outline and in substance, in intense colour. This is the time of life I am approaching. I shall collect my basket and ride my boat in this glory of evening, and be proud to be alive.

The Village

Ch—l

In Ch—l there are streets that wind around: a supermarket that resembles a metal bin; the faded town atelier, itself in need of repair; a 1930s art-nouveau lettered and designed post office with, incongruously, Joan of Arc on guard outside; a clean, refurbished market-place and church. What would it be like to live there, instead of my hamlet? What if there were unpleasant neighbours, what of the noise? The noise would not be constant, big city noise but sporadic, and therefore more perceptible. In the hamlet neighbours are spaced, shut behind hedges, separated by fields. How would town proximity affect me?

The pavillons on Ch—l streets are pretty, be-gardened, with tomatoes growing on high, twisted metal poles with marguerites between the rows, to avert insects. There are a few Swiss-chalet conceits. Most pavillons stand in the middle of green-and-gardened squares, but some spaces are rectangular or triangular. Usually the spaces are bordered by fence and shrub. The church sits plump in the market square, centred like the pavillons in their gardens. It has white hydrangeas around its base. Some streets lead to park areas with river, bridge and bench. One delightful semi-paved road runs along the railway line, two trains a day out and two in. The notaire has a huge house and park and there are several others in which largish families could escape the canaille.

In truth Ch—l inhabitants are farming, rather than city types. They wear rural clothing, caps, agricultural cover-alls. They exchange greetings and familiar stories – il faut rigoler. The cafés, on the whole, are rural – bistro rather than town – smart. The twice – weekly market and monthly fair sell local produce at a leisurely pace. One could write a book and print it while waiting to be served in the post office. There is a brass band that plays with great panache and esprit de corps on High days and holidays, which this town rigorously observes. On such days, the band breaks the peace of the church in forceful and joyful celebration. At concerts, as at services, people come and go in the church; God with them, croyant, they need not fuss about the rituals of entering His house.

So what would it be like to settle here, to wake and walk for a coffee and croissant, to take an apero, lingering on a terrace, unrestricted by the need to drive home? To be on hand for the High days? To have town gas, main drainage, a water supply that did not fail? But what would it be like to lose my separated, village space; green vistas; sky down to the tree line, space that does not end at next door's box plot? The sun, all day. My garden. Silence. Pas croyant myself, I assimilate sky and trees, wind, birds, crickets, sunrise. Some days I rarely speak; there is no need; there are no needs to fulfil; so much is happening in the silence. To voice a separate self is to distance this activity, this unity. The town can not compete; but it is good to visit.

Wild boar hunt

At 2.55 this afternoon they shot my wild boar. He was my wild boar because I saw him, big, brown and round, with a big belly, he was a circle with four spoke-legs and a huge, ugly, snouted head, with shaggy, dangling ears. I did not see the tusks. He leapt, surprisingly agile and graceful, from a forest path into the hedgerow, to hide. He was bigger than me but rightfully, mortally terrified of people. There is a stuffed boar's head in a local café, a boar shot by the licensee, in the pride of his marksmanship and the bravery of having stood his ground. He is a kindly man and boars destroy crops. There is open season on their hunting.

I told no-one about my boar. Previously, I told, I told of the beavers I had seen, wonderful smooth swimmers who cry like babies and dam the rivers. An old beaver watched me, head just out of his hiding place. A family sunned themselves on the grass bank, cleaning. The hunt massacred them.

So I told no-one about my boar. Nevertheless, watching, over the last three days, I saw cars parked by the forest paths, blocking escape routes. Today, just as my walk began, I saw a group of cars, some of which drove into the forest itself. Horns sounded, sharp, excited. Boar surrounded. I heard two shots at 2.50pm, then a furied frenzy of dog barking. Another half a kilometer, two more shots, shouting, yelping. Then moaning, calling, almost a mooing, yearning. Two more shots. Nearly home. A final seventh shot. Silence.

The Market

The market has met for centuries, on Tuesdays and Fridays, in the lee of the chateau. It is now a slight shadow of its former self; two butchers, two vegetable stalls, a chicken-and-egg stall, a bread and cakes van, the goats' cheese man, two fish stalls and sometimes flowers, or shoes, an African with handbags and Michael Jackson t-shirts. Once a Citroen dealer made his way here, mistakenly and to no profit; sometimes there are beds, and occasionally a chair-mender. Now and again there is a lorry selling tools and garden equipment, mechanical pieces, covers for log steres, ladders. When it is winter-cold and wet, the stalls form a half-circle, like wagons taking up position to ward off an Indian attack. Against the summer sun, the vegetable stall has a tent. Service is slow in all weathers, the object of the occasion being to meet and talk, not to buy in haste. Older men, after much deliberation, buy two fresh sardines, an artichoke, to eat raw with their lunch. The hotel bar boasts a small increase its usual share of customers, whose dwindling ranks are enhanced by the market habituées. These are mostly men, many in their seventies or eighties, some in their nineties. Born here of a hardy race, these small and compact men have spent their lifetime working with the land and its produce. Their hands, bent and twisted, their damaged backs and legs, the trifling coins in their pockets, are witness of hard labour, ill-paid. It is, however, their enemies of the Hundred Years' War who keep the market alive, paying its inflated prices. Whenever remotely possible the ex-pats sit on the hotel terrace in couples and quartets, summer men in shirt-sleeves and sunglasses, summer women in skimpy clothes that proclaim their foreignness as much as their unfortunate dress-sense.

Josette went to the market in the 1939-45 war, when the German troops were stationed in the town. She took eggs on a folded blanket, beneath which was hidden her shopping list. When she left her basket to walk round greeting her compatriots, distributing her eggs, her list would be discreetly fulfilled beneath the blanket. The Germans had named hostages at the start of their occupation. When the resistance won a nearby battle, killing German soldiers, these hostages were stood all day against a wall, while the mayor pleaded for their lives, arguing that his commune could not be held responsible for the delinquencies of another place. He finally won his argument; the two men killed were two of the three that fled the wall. The third escaped. Crosses mark the sites of the killings. Now the police prowl the market environs; they are only in town on Tuesdays and Fridays and they need their quota of arrests of those who have taken the wheel having drunk not wisely, but too well.

I go to the market on Fridays, to meet Jojo. I buy little; prohibitively priced, the produce has suffered from to the weather. I am too impatient to queue. I have, I think, as a Hundred-Year-War enemy descendant, been occasionally overcharged. I meet, however, many people. I have my round: the tobacconist for the lotto, television magazine, cigarettes and stamps; the baker; the bank and the post office. (I do not buy stamps in the post office because I do not have thirty minutes to spare in the queue.) Jojo is usually on the hotel steps: bisou, bisou, 'un café?' 'Bien sûr.' We climb the steps and enter, greeting the groups at the various tables, shaking hands or kissing cheeks. We sit opposite each other at a long table, on benches. 'Quoi de nouveau?' 'tout est vieux!' The patron is fond of Jojo, whom he calls 'Papi.' 'Papi' buys the first round, a kir-and-water for him, a coffee for me. My coffee is the dearer drink and his monthly income is very small, pocket-money given him by the maison de retraite, which took his small capital in exchange for his bed and board. He has, however, his capital of pride, so I accept my coffee. I buy the second round; the timing is difficult, not letting his glass stay empty too long, nor yet ordering too quickly, so that he has to hurry the precious liquid; not missing the presence of the patron, who is inclined to wander off. Then Jojo buys his sardines and I take him back to the maison de retraite. I could eat with him if I paid a small fee, but I decline his offer, because there is a glint in his eye that belies his 76 years, and that really is a problem too far.

I like to be with Jojo because he fondly remembers my husband, when he was in his prime. My husband's sudden death greatly moved Jojo, as it did most of those I meet, who came to his funeral and buried him with the consolation 'il a profité de la vie', which is true; though cut short, it was a life that made its mark. My husband helped many people, in his capacity as a trade union officer and because that was his character. Markets fascinated him. Having done his butcher's apprenticeship he knew Smithfield and greatly admired the bummarees, the male-club atmosphere, the pubs open early morning and all day. I remember us watching the dismantling of a sizeable English market, how he delighted in the way the canvas was taken down and folded, the rods stacked, the streets washed down. 'The fish stall is always the last to pack up,' he often told me. He once played football across a French market square with the fish-stall holder, as predicted the last survivor of a busy Saturday market. I remember a one-time English acquaintance, 'Dick the Fish,' marketer, holder of a hawker's licence, circus worker. A shady character if ever there was one, the quality of his marine produce was once praised, amazingly, in the *Daily Telegraph*. (We were nowhere near the sea, and where Dick got his fish was a secret between him and his Maker; as was whether he paid for it). Dick the Fish, who lived in a caravan, evaded the penalties for fifteen drink-driving arrests by the simple expedient of not turning up for court, and moving on. Unlike the market itself, its characters are transients, fleeting visitors to its age-old presence.

Life in France

You are who you speak. I found this in the Labour Party, the Trades Unions and my Oxford College, where my South London accent, oddly in some cases, was an asset. Uncompromising by default, I became strong. I was from the working class, of which people were a bit afraid. I could not be counted on to toe lines, or be polite. I might bite. Of course, I did not know I had an accent until I left South London, where everyone spoke like me.

My accent comes with me to France, but is subsumed by my Englishness. I am an exotic-stranger-cum-English-clown. I have no accent except English. I am classless. I do not farm.

The regional accent is strong. Twenty years ago, we were the only English people in our village and we learnt quickly. My husband, who did not study French at school, indeed learnt nothing much at all except how to box, does better than me. It is not only the language that we must learn, but what subjects to speak of, when to speak and when to stay silent, when to laugh.

I hear from a Canadian friend. Her father was a Jewish emigré from Poland, her mother English, but she was brought up in Anglophone Canada. When she marries a French Canadian, she must learn not only a language (French was frowned on at her Anglophone school) but a whole new French Canadian history, social life and religion. She is at first mute at gatherings of her husband's family. When she eventually tries to speak, with her husband translating, she is angry because she feels the meaning of her words is not conveyed. When she finally becomes fluent, she is hopeful that Canada's linguistic divisions will lose their importance, that everyone will speak both languages. I think she is optimistic.

The French we speak here in the Charente is not the original language of the region, which was Occitan. The Langue d'Oc stretched down to Spain and Italy in the time of the Troubadours. Richard Coeur du Lion never spoke Langue d'Oil, never mind English. Now, some patois remains, but it is rather a bastardisation of RP French than Occitan. Young people have their own speech mannerisms, one goes to a 'resto', the cat goes to a 'veto'. Language, as my Canadian friend learnt, is history, and is society.

Mary, an English friend who lives in the Charente, is going to sell her house and return to Wiltshire, because she cannot learn French sufficiently well to speak fluently. She says, 'we cannot handle our own problems,' she says 'it is only half a life.' She is right. If one cannot communicate fully, one is barred from fully living in France, by one's own deficiencies. The alternative is to live English-in-France, to socialise ex-pat. This is a dangerous and slippery road to travel. At the worst, one will be reduced to discussing washing machines and digital cameras and the woman on the till at Leclerc over too much wine at gatherings that have the feel of a wagon train huddled against the expected Indian attack.

This relates to what I have been thinking about identity. As a historian, I am interested in the triangulation between author, subject and reader. The identity of the subject changes as viewed by the author and experienced by the reader. Richard Coeur du Lion is a case in point, reinvented by Hollywood as the good guy, in the guise of Sean Connery. A Scots woman told me that the audience at a cinema in Glasgow stood and cheered when Connery, a Scottish Nationalist, appeared on the screen as Crusader and English king.

As authors, we write for a supposed readership, some of us for children. Perhaps we can, through our subjects, help to sketch in the other half of the missing life for the Anglophone French residents? Or am I being over-optimistic, like my Canadian friend? Will I always have an English head on the body rooted, now, in France? And for those of us, like Mary, who find juggling our thoughts and words too exhausting, is the answer to 'Go Back'? Having been away some time, assumed French habits and lifestyle, will she find she can still speak Wiltshire?

We Walk

We walk among our dead:
our brave and trusted friends
who fought the foe and lost;
our parents, siblings, spouse.

We walk among the dead:
the tortured, humbled, hurt;
the happy, sweet, the kind;
the surprised, at sudden ends.

We walk among the dead:
forebears, ancestral shades;
believers in religions lost,
who saw a different world,
a landscape green and forested,
a sea of dreams and sagas,
their lives quick, and scared, and gone.

We walk among the dead
buoyed up by their teeming presence,
our light fuelled by their glow,
our very faces and our corps,
our health and energy
shaped by their experience,
formed by their actions.

We are a cumulation,
we are the living witness of the past.

Louise Maigret and her Jules

The Maigret novels of Georges Simenon are set firmly in place – primarily Paris, seconded by Meung-sur-Loire, with occasional excursions to other venues in France or abroad, but they are not set firmly in time. The more recent television series have opted for the 1950s, which is right for perhaps half of the novels. In others, the presence of horse and carriage, gas lighting, heating by wood-burning stove point to the 1920s and '30s. Simenon started on the wrong foot when, in 1934 (*Le Commissaire Maigret*) he retired his hero and had him live at Meung, at a country cottage complete with stove, Madame Maigret donning her sabots to fetch the wood. Thereafter the time setting is deliberately vague. In *Les Mémoires de Maigret*, written in 1950 supposedly by Maigret himself, Simenon has him say: 'Je n'ai pas la mémoire des dates'. Maigret's age fluctuates. *La Première Enquête de Maigret*, written in 1948, sets this first enquiry in 1913, which would give him a date of birth of 1890 or so. However, he would have then have retired at the age of

44. Interestingly, some of the later novels (*L'Ecluse no.1*, 1977) are set in the pre-war period. In *L'Ecluse no.1* Simenon reverts to the original retirement date. Maigret never learns to drive. Madame Maigret does (*L'Ami de l'Enfance de Maigret*, 1968).

Madame Maigret is one of the enigmas of 20th century fiction. At first view she is a cipher, a Jill Archer from Alsace who superbly makes the quiche lorraine of her region. This effacement is the more surprising given the depth and variety of Simenon's female characters: prostitutes, brothel keepers, killers, maids, mistresses, policewomen, mothers, daughters are described in deft character sketches, showing, where appropriate, motive for crime or collaboration. Take for example Ginette, in *Mon Ami Maigret* (1949). We are told her past: a prostitute, living with a petty criminal, she had tuberculosis. When her boyfriend was imprisoned Maigret send her to a sanatorium, where she spent several years and was cured of her illness. Now she reappears, under-mistress of a brothel, because she is too scarred by her medical treatment for her old trade and unable to find other employment. Maigret, despite some initial suspicion of her motives, treats her almost as a colleague. Or there is the superb Félicie in her red hat and parrot-coloured clothes (*Félicie est là* 1941), a little mad and driving Maigret to distraction, but evoking his tenderness.

Of course, one of the reasons behind the mystery of Mme. Maigret is that she exists at all. Maigret is a policeman who goes home at night and sometimes at lunch-time to their apartment in the boulevard Richard Lenoir, who goes to Meung for weekends, visits the cinema and walks the boulevards of Paris with his wife, arm-in-arm, visits friends and has relatives to stay. He is not a lonely super-hero. When retired, he much enjoys his life: 'Il jouissait pleinement de cette retraite et de la maison qu'il avait amouresement aménagée' (*Maigret à New York*, 1946). He has always wanted a country life, to be where fruits are ripening, the hay is cut, and Mme. Maigret makes her ragouts. His long-time deputy Lucas visits, but they do not talk about the police. He misses the warm body of his wife when she is not in their bed (*Le Commissaire Maigret*). At night she wears her hair in pins at first, and then curlers. Her name is Louise (*Les Memoires de Maigret*), his names are Jules Amédée François (although Jules unaccountably becomes Joseph in *L'Ecluse no. 1*, where equally oddly they have moved from boulevard Richard Lenoir).

Louise Maigret is a tall woman, fresh-complexioned, who smells newly washed:

Elle sentait bon le frais et la savonette ... c'était une grosse fille fraiche comme on n'en voit que dans les pâtisseries ou derrière le comptoir de marbre des crémeries, une grosse fille plein de vitalité qu'il pouvait pourtant laissez les journées entières dans leur petit appartement ... sans qu'elle s'ennuyait un instant.

Louise is also blessed with *une qualité appreciable: elle était aussi fraiche, aussi enjouée à sa reveil qu'au mileu d'après-midi.* (*La Première Enquête*).

The Maigrets met when he first came to Paris (*Les Mémoires de Maigret*). Maigret was taken to the Friday night dances given by M. and Mme. Léonard, with whom their niece Louise, *la plus délicieuse des jeunes filles*, was staying. M. Léonard, and most of the other guests, were civil servants, working for the Ponts et Chaussées department, and looked down on the gauche Jules, who wore a uniform to work and, from discomfort in their salon, scoffed all the pastries. Louise, her expression *douce, rassurante, presque familière,* took pity on him and talked with him; she disliked dancing. Maigret never asked Louise to marry him; he took it for granted that she would. When her aunt asked his intentions, he went to see her parents and received permission to renew his request after a few months, during which time he and Louise were not to meet; he was allowed to write once a week. In later years the mere mention of the Ponts et Chaussées makes them smile at each other. However, beware: in *Les Mémoires* we are told that Louise likes the portrait Simenon draws of her, *toujours chouchotant son grand bébé de mari* but that, like all portraits, this is far from being exact. In *Maigret s'Amuse* (1956) Louise sulks for 15 minutes when Jules dares to remind her of a little wood, a week before their marriage. In *Les Scruples de Maigret* (1956) it is Louise who reminds Maigret of their first trip to the Opéra Comique, thee weeks after they met, and their first kiss, on the stairs. They saw Carmen, and Louise wore a blue taffeta dress, and very high-heeled shoes. Feigning to stumble, she laid her fingers on Maigret's arm, and he pretended not to notice. After that, she always took Maigret's arm when they walked together.

Of Louise's family we know the major names – Schoëller, Kurt, Léonard – and that they come from Colmar in Alsace, between Strasbourg and Mulhouse. It was a Kurt in the Napoleonic régime who established the Ponts et Chaussées. Louise has a married sister, whose birthday is the 19th October (*Maigret et l'Homme du Banc*, 1952) and who, with her husband André, visits the Maigrets every year. The visit always goes well for the first couple of days and then both Maigrets wish their visitors gone (*L'Ami de Maigret*). They play cards, Louise *riait à tout moment aux éclats parce qu'elle n'était jamais parvenu à connaitre les cartes et qu'elle faisait toutes les bêtises imaginables* (*L'Ombre Chinois*, 1963). The in-laws have a son, who finds he is unsuited to life as a policeman (Le Commissaire Maigret). The Maigrets holiday with her family in Alsace, except when a case ordinarily outside his jurisdiction tempts Maigret to a change of scene, as in *Au Rendezvous des Terres Neuvas* (1977).

The Maigrets had a daughter who died at birth, their only child. When a senior officer asks them when he can expect to fulfill his promise to be godfather to their baby, *il n'a jamais compris pourquoi nous rougissons, pourquoi ma femme baissait les yeux, tandis que j'essayais de lui toucher le main pour consoler.* The child born dead, and the death of the mother in childbirth are a recurring theme of Simenon's. Maigret's own mother died giving birth to the child who would have been Maigret's brother (*Les Mémoires*), his father having kept faith with a doctor who drank. The drunken doctor attending a chilbirth with fatal consequences reappears in *L'Ecluse no. 1*.

From the start, Louise's domain is the home, providing nourishment, rocking no boats. The apartment at first has no bathroom, just a tub, and for breakfast they have soup, as they would have had in the country. They did not expect to be long at boulevard Richard Lenoir, but stay their for 30 years, later buying the next door apartment to augment their space. Their domains are firmly separated; Louise would have liked to drive her big boy to work, but does not, in case they meet one of his colleagues. Her world ends exactly at the door of their apartment; she stuffs him into overcoats and scarves when he leaves for the big outdoors; on his return she always recognises his step, and opens the door for him, welcoming him back from his world into hers. Maigret loves their little rituals more than he will admit to himself:

sa femme avait un geste particulier pour lui prendre des mains son parapluie mouillé en même temps qu'elle penchait la tête pour l'embrasser sur la joue (Maigret Chez le Ministre, 1954).

If work comes in the door, in the form of colleague, or witness, Louise effaces herself. When she enters his world, seeing him on duty when shopping, as a young married woman, *c'était délicieuse* (*Les Mémoires*). She knows all his colleagues, and when he takes her to police headquarters one Sunday, she finds everything familiar, just as he had described it; her only comment, *c'est moins sale que j'aurais cru*. Louise has the vitality and the confidence to organise her own day, her own interests. Maigret never asks her how she spends her day. She is not, perhaps, overly intelligent; apart from housework, and daily shopping trips, we are told that she collects the stamps from a certain brand of café and puts them in albums; three complete albums would win her a bedroom set. However, we must remember she lives most of the time in the centre of Paris; she has only to leave the apartment to be spoilt for choice of occupation. Both Maigrets lean their elbows on their windowsill to watch the retreat with flambeaux from the Place de Bastille.

Notwithstanding their separate worlds, Louise does sometimes help in Maigret's enquiries. There is always a reason. At the time of his first enquiry, there is a female witness to guard and Maigret is a very junior policeman who cannot command the resources he would later have. Louise guards his female witness, night and day, and cooks for her. It is unusual that her intervention takes place on her ground, in their apartment. More often, if Louise becomes at all involved in one of his cases, it is on neutral ground. When Maigret shows her a letter he has received announcing a forthcoming murder (*Maigret Hésite* 1968) it is in a restaurant where they eat fruits de mer. For once she does not take his work seriously. In *Le Temoinage de l'enfant de choeur* (1956) Maigret is both ill and displaced, on enquiry in the provinces; she has accompanied him, unable to bear the thought of him eating in restaurants, and they have rented a furnished apartment. Their worlds have collided and Louise takes on an active role, going to the crémerie to telephone for him (there is no telephone in the lodging), taking messages, seeking witnesses and arranging for them to talk with Maigret. In *Maigret à Vichy* (1968) Jules, accompanied by Louise, is on holiday at Vichy, taking the waters for his health. They walk everywhere and her feet hurt; *ils ne s'asseyaient jamais*. Jules chooses the route. He reads the newspaper in the afternoon when she sleeps. Louise is worried that her husband will be bored, but he is not; it is she who is most displaced, away from their apartement. Maigret does solve a crime, and Louise allows him the space: *elle sentait son mari détendu, comme s'il existait une zone dans laquelle elle ne se reconnaissait pas le droit de pénétrer.* Her reward is that *qu'un contact plus intime s'éstablissent entre eux*; also, she hears more about the case than usual. At home she almost never hears about his cases, except once when he gets drunk, a rare occurrence (*Maigret et le Corps sans Tête*, 1955); he is alarmed and embarrased in the morning to realise how much he has said.

Louise's most active intervention is in L'*Amie de Mme. Maigret* (1949). On regular visits to the dentist, Louise meets a young woman whose identity later proves important. Louise, who never wears a watch, is tricked into minding the woman's child and is back late for lunch, something that has never happened before. The chicken is burnt. Maigret has never seen her in such a state, *le chapeau de travers, la lèvre agitée d'un tremblement*. Despite this, Louise takes it on herself to identify the woman by finding the boutique which sold her smart, white hat. This she feels is a job for a woman and she makes her feet sore patrolling Paris, looking for a shop which is neither for the very rich nor a chain store. She is successful and in large part this solves the case. This incursion into Maigret's domain affects Louise, temporarily changing her character: *il y avait dans sa voix une bonne humeur presque aggressive qu'il ne lui connaissait pas.* She is *triomphant et narquoise avec, malgré tout, un tremblement inquiet des lèvres.* They lunch on cold meats from an Italian delicatessen, which recalls for him the early years of their marriage when she delighted in finding such dishes; there is a sexual overtone; Maigret is having to newly appreciate his wife. She dares to remind him that he is rarely home for lunch. When he calls to ask her to meet him for an evening meal and to visit the cinema (the leopard has not entirely changed his spots; he wants to see a police message he has issued for the newsreel), she says *Si tu es sûr que tu seras libre. Sûr, sûr? C'est trop beau pour être vrai et je prevois que tu vas rappeler ici une heure pour m'annoncer que tu rentras pas ni dîner ni coucher.* What price the trembling lips now?

Similarly, Maigret sometimes enters Louise's world. In *Maigret s'Amuse*, other plans having fallen through, they end up on holiday in Paris. It s neither a Sunday, nor is Maigret ill; he enjoys watching *le rythme de journées da sa femme*. They go adventuring together, lunching and dining in little restaurants. In this situation, it is Jules who looses his identity rather than Louise: *Même pour elle, il n'était pus tout à fait Maigret, maintenant quil n'allait pas au Quai des Orfèvres.*

Their relationship is thus not a static one. Louise and Jules were newlyweds at the time of his first big case (*La Première Enquête*). She laughed to see him in bed, sleepy-eyed: *elle riat toujours quand elle s'approchait du lit le matin, une tasse de café à la main et qu'il regardait avec des yeux vagues et un peu enfantin.* At this time Louise still called her husband Jules, but she honoured him as she did her father, as she would have honoured a son: *elle avait déjà pour lui cette sorte de respect que lui était propre, le même qu'elle avait du vouer à son père, le même qu'elle vouerait à son fils, si elle en avait un.* Proud of her husband, she could give him a gentle hint; when he put on an inappropriate jacket to go to an evening party, *quelque chose indéfinissable dans son accent, dans sa sourire, ... lui avertissait de ne pas essayer de se faire passer pour un jeune clubman.* Maigret at this time hung his shaving mirror up in the kitchen so that he could be with her, watch her in the morning.

Later, *depuis toujours, peut-être parce que une fois ils l'avaient fait en riants, ils s'appelaient Maigret et Madame Maigret* (*Le Temoinage de l'Enfant de Choeur*). She has come to know Maigret's faults, his obstinacy: *Sachant par expérience qu'il était inutile de contrarie son gros homme de mari* and that illness made him bad-tempered, she refuses him his pipe, makes tisanes, has her box of medicines handy. Maigret indulges his taste for tobacco when Louise is out; she knows, but refrains from comment: *Qui sait si elle ne soupçonnait pas le coup de rhum?* As they grow older, they are grateful for their long comradeship:

Or dans les regards ... il y avait de la nostalgie et de la reconnissance. "Pourquoi exiger que le reste du monde demeure immobile alors que nous veillisons?" C'était çela ... qu'ils disent d'un batement de paupières, et ils se disent aussi merci (Maigret s'Amuse).

In *Les Scruples de Maigret* it is Louise who feels herself unfit, out of breath when climbing the stairs and feeling a heaviness in her legs. She goes to see their old friend Dr. Pardon, swearing him to secrecy (he immediately telephones Maigret). Pardon prescribes pills and that she looses some weight. Maigret goes looking for her pills, which he cannot find, and is saddened by the undeniable fact that they are both growing older, like old cars that have to be left in the garage most of the time. To Louise's great chagrin, he suggests that they take a maid. Offended at what she takes to be an assault on her domain, she asks if the dinner is poor. He takes her to the cinema, buys her sweets, and finds that she has already lost weight and appears more fragile. He is frightened that she will lose her customary good humour. By the 1960s, the Maigrets are driving into the countryside for Sunday lunch, Louise timid at the wheel, and have bought a television (*L'Ami de l'Enfance de Maigret*). Despite having promised themselves to watch only the interesting programmes, within a fortnight they have changed their places at the dining table so that both can watch while eating.

Childless, having no relatives in Paris (presumably the Ponts and Chaussées brigade has died out or moved on), the Maigrets are a very solitary couple. This makes more credible Louise's devotion to Maigret and his job; there is no competitor for her affections. As if to compensate for their restricted social life, Simenon introduces the Pardons in the 1950s, with whom the Maigrets visit once a month, returning the hospitality, so that they have a fortnightly dinner. Louise and Madame Pardon knit and talk; Pardon sometimes gives Maigret insight into characters and their motivation. When the Pardons' daughter is pregnant, Louise is to be godmother (*Une Confidence de Maigret*, 1959). In *Maigret et les Viellards* (1960), the Pardons make a change, inviting their friends to dinner in a restaurant on the boulevard du Montparnasse, where all four eat on the terrace. Louise is worried that she is too old to wear her flowered dress. The restaurant proves to be the one at which the Maigrets first dined alone together; the menu has not changed, and they order the same dishes.

What purpose does Louise serve Simenon? Most of the action of a Simenon story comes in the last few pages; never go to bed with a Simenon to finish, because these last pages require careful reading and reflection. There is very little action in the main body of the tale. Simenon knew this, and tells us in *Les Memoires de Maigret* that he is content, for instance, to let one policeman carrying out one stretch of observation stand in for the many that would have been necessary in a given case. The plot has thus been worked out leisurely, without fuss. It lies in nuances of character, a badly lit stair, a doorbell, a sound half-remembered, half-seen things whose importance is revealed in a few final words.

It is in these nuances that Louise is important; it is often through her agency that we half-see, half-hear. She is often crucial to Maigret's understanding of the case he is dealing with; for example, in *Les Scruples de Maigret* it is by comparing the wife of the chief suspect, and their relationship, with his own that Maigret seizes the truth. Apart from the occasions mentioned when Louise makes a direct involvement with the enquiry, it is her personality, her habits, which throw into relief those of the criminal or victim. In *Au Rendezvous des Terres Neuvas* Louise, despite being deprived of her usual family holiday and far from her Paris apartment, makes the best of a bad job with her sewing and knitting, even looking after the suspect's fiancée. She is in sharp contrast to the obstinate woman who insisted on being taken on a fishing boat where, despite being hidden in the captain's cabin, her presence led to a chain of events including murder and false arrest. In *Maigret à Vichy* Louise, wholly married, is contrasted to the murderous Hélène Longe, who lives alone at Vichy, seemingly self-sufficient in the floating population. The clue to the crime is that Hélène is less independent than she appears; her sister has had a baby, put out to nurse in the Vosges, who drowned. The sisters have been blackmailing the baby's father. Similarly, the Maigret home setting contrasts with the masculine one of the police headquarters and the Brasserie Dauphine. It is at home that Maigret plays out his feelings about a case, heavy and obsessed, or jovial and playful, sleeping well or sleeping badly. This saves Simenon pages of explanation and dialogue; he can place Maigret at home, conjure up his mood in a few words, relying on his readers to know when these differ from the ordinary, and we enter into Maigret's feelings. We can then watch him put on his eternal overcoat and go out to solve the crime.

Lady Audley's Revenge

In reply to Mary Elizabeth Braddon' s 'Lady Audley's Secret' (1860)

For the uninitiated: In Mary Elizabeth Braddon's Victorian sensation novel, Helen Maldon, daughter of a drunkard naval officer and a mentally-ill mother, reared in poverty, marries soldier George Talboys. His father cuts off his allowance and, desperate before their poverty, he leaves wife and baby to seek his fortune in Australia, leaving a note but otherwise making no contact for three years. Helen changes her name to Lucy Graham and works as a governess. She meets, and bigamously marries, Sir Michael Audley, a rich country squire nearly forty years her senior. Within months George, who has indeed made his fortune, returns to England. Warned of his imminent arrival by a newspaper article, Helen/Lucy fakes her own death. George is devastated and goes to St Petersburg with his friend Robert Audley, Sir Michael's nephew and the unlikely hero of the novel, a barrister who does not practise but lives on the allowance made to him by his uncle. On their return Robert and George visit

Sir Michael, staying at an inn. George sees Helen/Lucy at her carriage window and goes alone, without telling anyone, to meet her. She attacks him and he falls down a well. She thinks he is dead. His sudden disappearance is a mystery Robert determines to solve. The main part of the novel is devoted to Robert's attempts to find George and then, convinced he has been murdered, to build a chain of evidence leading to the murderer, who is gradually revealed to be Lucy. In an attempt to avoid exposure, Lucy sets fire to an inn where Robert is staying. Robert, however, escapes, although the innkeeper is badly burnt and dies in a few weeks, not entirely due to the arson but also because of his drunkenness. Faced by the evidence of her guilt, Lucy pleads insanity. Robert calls a doctor, whose opinion is that Lucy is not mad, but has dangerous insane moments; nevertheless, Lucy is sent to an asylum in Belgium, under the name of Mrs. Taylor: in effect a sentence of life imprisonment without appeal. Robert alone has evidence that the inn fire was arson, and he does not reveal this, in order to save his uncle pain. The suspected murder of George is more widely known. Robert marries George's sister Clara and brings up their son together with Helen and George's boy. George is revealed to be alive, having escaped from the well and spent a year in America, and joins Robert and Clara's household. Robert writes briefly to Helen to inform her that George Talboys is alive and well. His experiences have transformed Robert, who becomes a successful barrister and is heir to Sir Michael. After a year, Robert is informed by the asylum of Mrs. Taylor's death.

Lady Audley, now Mme. Taylor, remained in a torpor for perhaps three days after being confined by her husband's nephew, Robert Audley to the Belgian Maison de Santé. The same fate that had met her mother had befallen her; life imprisonment in a mad-house. The young woman who had been hired to wait on her pitied her, and tried to rouse her from her indifference by brushing her golden hair, praising its fairy texture, producing Madame's own little stock of cosmetics, in their jewelled cases, to assist her complexion, and telling her the gossip at the Maison. Gradually the lethargy passed; Mme. owned to the first name of Hélène. She spoke French prettily, with an English accent but perfect grammar. After a fortnight she received a letter from Robert Audley, which she wept over and hid in her bosom.

Warming to her young maid Solange, Hélène gave her money to buy chocolates, which they ate one by one with their coffee, made to perfection by Solange on the little spirit lamp in Hélène's room. When she was sure of Solange's loyalty, Hélène determined on taking the first step towards freedom. Drawing from her bosom Robert's letter which informed her that George Talboys was alive and well, Hélène asked Solange to make a fair copy, and to take both copy and original to the notaire. He was to keep the original in his safe, and return the notarised copy. Solange was given an item of the precious porcelain that Hélène had brought secreted in her luggage, with which to pay the notaire. Solange brought back both the fair copy and the porcelain, the notaire having said that he felt it an honour to serve the fair lady described to him, and hoping, perhaps, for future profit from her continued custom. Being blessed with a fine gift of impersonation, Solange entertained her mistress with an account of his solemn utterances.

Little by little Hélène recovered her looks, and even the ghost of her girlish laugh. She was docile and polite, and occasionally, through Solange, provided patisseries for the matron, the resident principal doctor, M. Dessais, and the wife and children of the director, Dr. Val. In return, she was asked to join not merely the communal, frugal dinner of the patients, but the monthly dinner parties the matron gave for local dignitaries, including the notaire and the bank manager. Both of these worthies had had occasion to make short-term use of the Maison for family members and clients troubled by their own relatives. More than one baby born to an unwed mother had met the world in its discreet bedrooms. More than one rich and ancient relative had left the world in similarly hushed surroundings. Adulterous wives had found shelter in its walls while awaiting exile to foreign climes; beautiful mistresses had been pampered while their establishments were being furnished. Neither notaire nor bank manager had thus reason to suspect that the youthful, innocent-looking, beautiful Hélène Taylor was confined because of suspected murderous insanity. The notaire made a fuss of Mme. Taylor on their first meeting, assuring her that her business was safe in his hands. Having read Robert's brief note, brought him by Solange and kept securely in his safe, he assumed that poor Mme. Taylor had had an unfortunate relationship which had been terminated by a jealous husband by falsely informing her of her lover's death. The bank manager, not slow to follow the notaire's lead, promised pretty Mme. Taylor a warm welcome and his personal attention if she should visit his premises.

After a very few weeks, Hélène was allowed small holidays from the Maison, accompanied by Dr. Dessais, to buy her patisseries herself, and to purchase wool and silk for her embroidery and watercolours for her sketches. The best of these showed a tall, handsome dragoon, with just a suggestion of his horse in the background. Her room was brightened by her own needlework and art and by the addition of a few of the treasures she had secretly brought from her English home. Those on display were by no means the richest which, again through the services of Solange, were safely deposited at the bank. The manager made it his duty, at the monthly dinners, to assure Mme. Taylor that her treasures were safe in is hands.

Meanwhile, Robert Audley's establishment had been enriched by the arrival of Sarah Covington as governess for the two boys. She had been found, after extensive advertising, by George Talboys. Coming back from Australia he had met Sarah on board ship, returning to her English fiancé after having worked for fifteen years as a governess abroad. She had been fearful of the future, he had been sanguine. While George's hopes had been dashed, Sarah's pessimism had proved ill-founded. If her fiancé had had amorous adventures, these were never revealed, and he had prospered in banking. He had, in truth, been surprised to hear of the return of his first love but, an easy-going man, not averse to the savings she brought as dowry, and mindful of the money gifts from her he had received over the years, he hid his astonishment and gracefully accepted an early marriage as inevitable. In fact, he had begun to find the pursuit of available women arduous and his bachelor establishment a trifle bleak. He had been pleasantly surprised by the governess's fifteen-year suppressed passion and its outcome, a beautiful little girl. Sarah Covington and her husband were installed in a cottage in the Audley household grounds. Mary, the little girl, was soon the favourite playfellow of both young George Talboys and Christopher Audley. Sarah Covington, who had no financial need to work, was welcomed in the household on an equal basis, and was held spellbound when Robert and George told of their adventures. She had more sympathy for Lucy Graham, whose difficult life as a governess she could imagine, than she revealed to Robert and George.

Some such sympathy for Hélène began to be felt not only by Dr. Dessais and the matron of the Maison de Santé, but also by its principal, Dr. Val. He had expressly been told by Robert that he was to treat his unwilling, anonymous guest with tenderness and compassion and that no expense should be spared for her comfort. Furthermore, he had been informed that she was not mad, but had 'inherited the seeds of madness from her mother and had given some signs of the taint.' Now Dr. Val was a progressive who doubted that madness could be inherited in such a way; in his view, madness would either be present and reveal itself continually or absent. As Hélène recovered from the trauma of her long pursuit by Robert Audley, the nightmare journey to Belgium and her confinement, she began to recover the sunny temper she had exhibited, as Lucy Graham, when governess in the Dawson household. Dr. Val came to the conclusion that if there was a taint, it had skipped a generation, and that Hélène was as sane as he.

Hélène gradually revealed a version of her past to Dr. Val. She told how Robert had pursued her, buying her expensive presents, such as her sables, telling her that George Talboys was dead. In this version, she cast herself as the grieving widow, who refused for a long time to believe in George's death. Finally convinced, she had lived for a short while under Robert's protection, giving credence to his promise of marriage in seven years' time, when George's death could be legally assumed. Then Robert had betrayed her with Clara Talboys and it was grief at this that had caused her breakdown. Seeking to protect Clara from the truth, Robert had arranged her confinement in Belgium; he then took her child from school and was bringing the little boy up as his own. This tale was prettily told, with much anguish expressed at her own betrayal of her husband and fall from virtue. It was convincing, uttered in broken accents from under a cloud of the fairy-gold hair, her docile deportment evidence of becoming resignation in the face of her present position as penance for having priced her love before her good name. It was supported by the fact that Robert had imprisoned her without revealing her true identity, so that her marriage to his uncle remained unknown to Dr. Val. It was supported by Dr. Val's own enquiries; Robert Audley had indeed married Clara Talboys and was bringing little George up as his own; George was alive and living in Robert's household. Hélène asked Dr. Val to treat her confessions with confidence, out of respect for the virtuous woman Robert had married. When, in time, she came to show Robert's letter to Dr. Val, asking him to forward it to Dr. Musgrave, on whose word she had been confined, to see if it altered Dr. Musgrave's opinion, Dr. Val readily assented. He did not reveal Hélène's story, merely relating that facts had come to his knowledge that rendered suspect Robert's part in the affair. The reply was not long coming. Dr. Musgrave's opinion was indeed changed. He had not, at first, supposed Lady Audley to be suffering from mental illness and now viewed Hélène's fearful agitation, on the one occasion he met her, as the result of false charges brought against her by Robert whom, from the first, he had regarded with some suspicion. Dr. Musgrave recalled that he had not thought Robert entirely frank with him. Robert was now living comfortably with the man Hélène had been accused of murdering, married to that man's sister. It seemed that Hélène might have been the victim of a conspiracy, disinherited by a much older husband, to Robert Audley's eventual benefit.

Robert was sent a copy of Dr. Musgrave's opinion and found himself in grave difficulty. He had accused Hélène of murdering a man to whom there was no evidence that she had been formerly married, and who was very much alive. He stood to inherit a huge amount of money and a country estate because of her confinement. Because he had wanted at all costs to save his uncle from the scandal of a public trial, Robert had told no-one of Hélènès supposed arson attempt, when he deduced that she had locked him in his room at the inn she caused to burn. The innkeeper had died, not just from his burns but also his drinking. From his legal experience, Robert knew that he had made of himself an accomplice after the event. A trial now would spell his ruin as surely as it would have spelt his uncle's. No-one would trust a lawyer who had kept quiet about arson from family pride. At the worst, he would risk a penalty of imprisonment. He could not therefore now reveal these addition grounds as

107

confirmation of Hélène's madness. The only witness to the arson was Hélène's once devoted maid, Phoebe. Robert was of the opinion that Phoebe would go to the grave with her secret. She was pleased to be rid of her brute of a husband; the insurance paid had put her finances on a sound footing; and having accompanied Hélène to the inn on the fateful night, Phoebe also faced possible conspiracy charges.

Dr. Val agreed that Hélène should be allowed to leave his establishment on a daily basis, provided that she was accompanied by her faithful Solange, and that she be made a small allowance. Hélène was always back in good time, always with small gifts of patisserie or flowers. She attended the Protestant church twice every Sunday and soon added the clergy, loud in praise of her piety and her small gifts to the poor, to her band of admirers. She frequently visited the bank and was bowed into the manager's office where, over sherry, she would deposit some of her jewellery and porcelain to be sold on her behalf. The bank manager was assiduous on her behalf and before very long, Hélène had amassed a little fortune. The banker helped her to buy and furnish a small house; Hélène had determined to run a school on her release, which she now viewed, with justification, as being imminent. Dr. Val was increasingly perturbed that he had been tricked into confining a woman who was evidently sane. Also, a certain noble Belgian family had need of her set of rooms for a mentally deficient princess. After a twelvemonth, he wrote to Robert Audley, falsely informing him of Mrs. Taylor's death. Robert, relieved, made no further enquiries. George Talbot wept a little on hearing the news. So did Sir Michael Audley, the man she had bigamously married. His health was failing, and he wished to be at peace with the world. He made a handsome settlement on little George, and added a codicil to his will, to the effect that his erstwhile wife, Lucy, had gone abroad after they parted; that the parting had been his fault, and that no stain should attach to her character. Lucy/Hélène was free.

The little house Hélène had bought in the suburbs of Brussels had been run as a school by an English woman, more than fifty years before. The rumour was that it had been bought for her by her lover and that, believing him to have perished at sea, she wrote her memoirs. Whatever the truth of this rumour, the Englishwoman had married a Professor Erasmus in her mid-thirties and had closed her school. Extending the accommodation, they had lived in the little house, then in the countryside, until their deaths a decade ago. The school equipment was still available, desks and chairs, slates and board. It suited Hélène to perfection. From the old registers she was able to contact some former pupils, now grandparents of hopeful offspring. These they were charmed to send to the new English governess, so much prettier and more gay than their own former teacher, but equal in rigour of discipline and breadth of knowledge. The English system, they told each other. With references from the bank manager and notaire, Hélène soon had her full complement of pupils. Even Dr. Val sent his granddaughter, perhaps eager to appease his former detainee. For ten years Hélène kept her school and profited therefrom. The skills of painting and embroidery she imparted, the proficiency her pupils gained in English and French, the style they acquired at the piano, ensured her success. Just as important to the project were her beauty and her pleasant manner, her girlish laughter and her fairy gold hair. Solange became an assistant mistress. Hélène's girls, carrying their accomplishments lightly, charmingly erudite, were proved to be eminently marriageable. Their little sisters soon followed in their steps.

It was Sir Michael Audley's death that prompted Hélène's next move. Wills were open to inspection, and she arranged that Sir Michael's was examined. The codicil he had added finally cleared her name. Hélène decided to return to London and to claim the inheritance she thought was her due, after years of suffering. She would defy Robert Audley, or George Talboys, to raise the old question of her bigamous marriage; they had no proof, and she has the attested certificate of Helen Talboy's death and her grave. She determined to take London by storm. Her economies, carefully invested by her banker, were sufficient to pay her way. So it was that Robert, Clara, George and his son, attending the opera, saw that a box near theirs was attracting considerable attention. George the younger, now a handsome young man in his eighteenth year, went to join the crowd watching the neighbouring box, and reported that it held a beautiful golden-haired woman, dressed in the height of fashion, speaking French. Leaning out, Robert saw, to his horror, that a phantom had appeared.

Robert pleaded sudden illness and took his party home. His feverishness, and confinement to his room for the following two days, supported his claim of ill health, but he refused medical treatment. Robert knew not what to do. He was standing for parliament, and any scandal would finish his chances. Dr. Val's attestation of Hélène's death could not be revoked without ensnaring Robert in charges of false imprisonment. Robert, after assiduously following the law for a decade, and making his name, had been reverting to his old indolent ways. He had seen a parliamentary seat as the ideal way of remaining in touch with affairs while partially retiring from his busy practice. He had thought that Sir Michael's inheritance would keep him and his family in easy circumstances for the remainder of his life. His only hope lay in persuading Lucy/Hélène to withdraw, by sacrificing some of that inheritance, and it was a very poor and fragile hope.

Hélène, meanwhile, was having the effect on London society for which she had hoped. She was seen everywhere, and no hostess felt her party complete if Mrs. Taylor was not among the guests. Mrs. Taylor's soirées at her hôtel, with her companion Solange, were the fashionable place to be seen. Soon Hélène began dropping hints of a difficult past, a rupture from her noble husband following a misunderstanding, brought about by a nephew whose evil scheme it was to trick her out of her inheritance. These hints made Hélène's society the more sought after and were embroidered by her auditors until the nephew became a monstrous character. Hélène talked freely about the school she had kept, and her bravery was admired as much as her beauty. It was seen that visiting Belgian notables sought out Mrs. Taylor, and more than one French Count whose daughters had been educated by the wise, chaste, well-informed teacher. Indeed, her beauty had matured, and on occasion she looked magnificent.

Robert remained in the toils of indecision and torment until young George returned one day to report that he had met with the beautiful Mrs. Taylor at a party, and fond her charming. Hs eulogies were so many thorns in Robert's flesh. Hélène had, quite naturally, ensnared her own son. Robert kept the secret of Mrs. Taylor's identity and return from Clara and George. The latter, he feared, would succumb to her just as easily as he had formerly admired the so-called Lucy Audley. As for Clara, content with the present, full of hope for the future, she hated to be reminded of the trials of the past. The only person to whom Robert could unburden himself was Sarah Covington. She was a good listener, but could see no way of exposing Hélène without ruining both Robert and his household.

So it was that Robert Audley was ushered in to Mrs. Taylor's suite of rooms. She saw a pleasant looking man, with little hair but a greatly increased waistline; the young man who had troubled her dreams a little over a decade before had vanished behind the signs of prosperity and a contented family life. He saw a slim, beautiful woman, assured and grander than the fascinating creature for whom he had once brought sables from Russia. It was Hélène who took charge of the conversation. She was gracious and offered refreshment. He was afraid. Hélène informed him, quite simply, that she was seeking legal advice on how to obtain the inheritance she was sure Sir Michael would want her to have. She asked Robert if legal proceedings would indeed be necessary or whether, if she did not take steps to sue him for false imprisonment and the money he had already spent while she worked for a living, they could arrive at an understanding. Robert agreed to think this over and to let her have an answer within a month. Hélène then proposed that her son should be introduced to her. At this, Robert leapt to his feet but the words of denial he formed did not issue from his lips. Instead, he made a promise to reveal to young George that the beautiful Mrs. Taylor was his mother, and to abide by the young man's wishes as to a meeting.

Robert returned home tormented by his position. He had endless discussions with Sarah; their intimacy, of which his wife was jealous, were the first signs of trouble in his household. Sarah was opposed to any exposure of Hélène, for young George's sake. After two weeks of worry and indecision, Robert finally told George and Clara of the return of the former Lady Audley. It was agreed between them, regretfully, that young George should be told that the beautiful Mrs. Taylor was his mother, but his father insisted that as the parent, and former husband, he should first meet Helen. Their meeting was arranged, at her hotel. George entered her suite hesitantly. He had always been worried by her imprisonment, and had mourned her supposed death. He had long ago forgiven her for her part in his adventures and borne the burden of his own guilt, in leaving her lonely, with a child and dissolute father. He was prepared to accept the results of her attack upon him, over a decade ago, as an accident. When he beheld the glorious creature who received him, he was speechless; when Helen knelt at his feet and begged his forgiveness for the past, he raised her up and swore that it should never again be mentioned between them. Thereafter he was a regular visitor to her rooms, a regular companion for her visits to the theatre and the opera, and was soon as nearly besotted as he had been on meeting her for the first time. It was due to George's insistence that Helen's meeting with their son should take place in his own home, Robert Audley's household.

This household was sadly changed from the peaceful abode it had been just a few months before. Clara was disturbed not just by Robert's frequent conversations with Sarah, but by George's renewed bewitchment. She sought to understand the past, to re-examine the chain of events, to convince herself of Helen's guilt. Clara was also anxious that her own son should not fall under Helen's spell. Sarah was fearful that the happy home in which she and her husband were settled might break up; she had hoped to raise her little girl in all the comfort and independence she and her husband could not afford. Sara's husband was disturbed because she was disturbed. Robert was ill from worry. He resigned all thought of a parliamentary career, but was unable to work. He became rather slovenly. Against this background, young George was introduced to the 'pretty lady' of his youth, and the goddess of his eighteenth year, as his mother. From then on, he worshipped her. His happiest hours were spent in her company, and long-buried memories of his childhood were reawakened. He began to view Robert with suspicion, remembering it was Robert who had taken him away from his grandfather and put him to school, where he had spent some miserable years.

The month Helen had given Robert for reflection was long over, having been extended by him on various legal excuses, until no more remained. Helen now set her terms; she claimed all of the inheritance; she would make a settlement on Robert equivalent to that generous pension which his uncle had made him in the days of his bachelorhood. She would draw up a will, leaving everything to young George and a small legacy to his half-bother Christopher. Try as he might, Robert could not find these conditions unreasonable, unless he broadcast truths that would spell his ruin. Eventually, they were agreed. A brother lawyer was brought in and a settlement drawn up. The hardest part for Robert was to attend the soirée at which Helen Taylor announced her reclaimed identity to society. Society was charmed. Lady Lucy Audley was reborn, and returned to live at Audley court.

So life continued for a number of years, but Lady Audley's revenge was not complete. Robert still had an independent existence, and she perhaps regretted the generosity of her settlement upon him. Also, life at the Court could be lonely. Solange was there for company, and so was Phoebe, who had returned to her former mistress. For these two, the day was hardly long enough for the machinations undertaken to usurp the other in Lady Audley's favour. Male company, however, was lacking. George visited but tended to sit and sigh wistfully at the might-have-been. Clara would not visit. Christopher accompanied young George on frequent visits, but never fell under Lady Audley's spell, despite her best endeavours. Young George was running up debts in London, banking on his future inheritance. Eventually his father took him and Christopher abroad, to his old haunts in Australia and America. There was enough of his father's adventurous spirit of former years to make this journey acceptable to young George, and his health benefited from leaving behind what had become rather a dissolute life in London. Christopher gave promising signs of having a good business brain, and looked fair set to make himself a fortune.

Soon thereafter, a second tragedy befell Robert Audley's sadly changed household. His wife Clara, never fully recovered from the destruction of her peace, gave birth to a seven-month child; neither mother nor baby survived. Sarah and her husband had moved out to establish their own independent lives, free from the disturbances that they feared would affect their beautiful daughter, and free from the corrupting influence of Lady Audley, which they had seen at work on young George. After a decent period, Lady Audley called Robert to her side; she suggested that they marry, so that he might enjoy the benefits of her inheritance (without, however, an increased allowance). Broken and lonely, incapable of work, Robert agreed, on one condition: that Lady Audley did not seek to deepen the intimacy with her son, or to persuade him to return from abroad. This

113

condition was acceptable to Lady Audley who had, in truth, begun to find the young man's enthusiasm and attention rather wearisome. So they lived together, not unhappily; Robert accepted his fate, the only sign of disquiet being that he was careful to go nowhere near the well. Lady Audley's revenge was complete.

Epilogue

The Election of God

And so it came about that men decided to put God up for election. He did not have a good track record – the Great Fire of London, The New Orleans tornado, slavery, famine, the crusades – but lately He seemed to be really laying it on a bit thick, war, famine and pestilence all over the globe. The Four Horsemen were so busy that the horses never saw their stables, and their shoes were a disgrace. It was quite difficult to know who to stand against God; any other immortal being, the Devil, Jesus, the Holy Ghost, were God so that was no use. Buddha declined on the grounds of being otherwise engaged, meditating. So people put forward all sorts of suggestions: their Aunt Wyn, their cats and dogs, a favourite spider, wild boar, elephants, Germaine Greer, Maigret, various Sylphs and Stags, Gandulf, Mohammed, Confucius, Father Christmas etc. Pigs suggested the Bandsman. Miranda was sure Derek would fulfil the role to perfection. Voting went on in people's heads and the results were posted on church doors. Hardly anyone except some of the clergy (those who did not vote for their boyfriend or favourite choirboy) voted for God Who was an overall loser. He had, of course, foreseen the outcome and had already made his way to the Garden of Eden, where He had wanted to reside for some centuries, and where He spent his time eating apples, kicking the serpent and toying with the idea of Adam and Eve mark 2.

Discounting people who had never existed in flesh and blood, like Maigret, or who were dead, like Mohammed, there remained very many living beings in each country who tied for first place. Britain was much the same as elsewhere: Aunt Wyn and Germaine Greer were elected along with a few thousand cats and the spider, who had made much of the early running. Dogs had tended to upset their owners before final voting, whereas cats had thoughtfully retired until it was all over. They knew they were God anyway. A Godhead Council of all the winners was called by the government, which had gone along with the election because of the photo-opportunities presented outside the church doors, taking down the lists for counting and looking wise. The Prime Minister had a new suit for the occasion. It was also one in the eye for the bishops.

However, not all the winners presented themselves. Many cats had rather lost interest. So Aunt Wyn and Germaine Greer were the most vocal and the others tended to leave them to get on with it. Someone stood on the spider. Very soon, Germaine Greer retired from the Council to write a book about it all, so that left Aunt Wyn. She sped about the country night and day, trying to be everywhere at once, a trick that God, still sulking in Eden, refused to impart. After a twelvemonth Aunt Wyn succumbed to a heart attack. The cats struggled on without her for a bit, but a cat does not live forever, so eventually a few bedraggled elephants and wild boars went to Eden to ask God to come back. Having foreseen this also, God received them very graciously. However, He also saw that while he was in Eden there had actually been less of war and famine, and the four Horsemen were very reluctant to come out of retirement. So God said every living thing that wanted could come to Eden with him, He would make it large enough, and those who wanted to stay in the world could do so, as long as they did not trouble Him.

~ The End ~

About the Author

Born and raised in London, Christine Collette now lives in rural South West France, in a stone cottage restored by her husband. Before settling in France ten years ago she had lived in Oxfordshire, Wiltshire and Lancashire, where she taught history and women's studies at Edge Hill University. A life-long trades unionist, she studied at Ruskin College and then Corpus Christi and St. Hugh's Colleges at Oxford. She has published extensively in the fields of Labour History and Women's Studies. Since her husband's death in 2008 she has concentrated on writing fiction, and also teaches English as a volunteer at her local Université de Temps Libre.

A note about Lady Audley's Revenge

The work is after the Radio 4 serial. There was also a film, released 17 May 2000. For more info, search for 'lady audleys secret' at

www.flixster.com   or   www.moviesplanet.com

'Lady Audley's Secret' is available as ebook and a Penguin Classic.

Publication History

'Weather Report from France', Countryside Tales Summer 2010 issue 42; 'The Dream' and 'The Market' Cherrystones The Writers' Group, Civray, 2011; Forthcoming, 'Rupert's Triangle' in Rich Pickings Chapter One Promotions, runner up in the 2011 International Short Story competition.

Academic: *The Newer Eve: Women, Feminists and the Labour Party* (Palgrave MacMillan, 2009); *British History 1979 – 2000: A Commentary and Reader* (I.B. Tauris,2003), with Keith Laybourn; *European Women's History: A Reader* (Taylor and Francis, 2001), with Fiona Montgomery; *Jews, Labour and the Left* (Ashgate, 2000), edited with Stephen Bird; T*he International Faith: Labour's Attitudes to European Socialism, 1918 –1939* (Ashgate,1998); *Into the Melting Pot: Teaching Women's Studies in the New Millennium* (Ashgate,1997), with Fiona Montgomery; *For Labour and For Women: the Women's Labour League, 1906 –1918* (Manchester University Press,1989);

Chapters and articles: *Friendly spirit, comradeship and good-natured fun: adventures in socialist internationalism between the wars* , International Review of Social History, 2003; *Women and Politics* in Chris Wrigley (ed.), Blackwell's Companions to British History: the Early Twentieth Century' (Blackwell, 2003); *The Limits of Common Interest* in the International Federation of Trades Unions, 1919 –1939; ACTA, International Conference: *The Past and Future of International Trades Unionism*, (IALHI /AMSAB 2002); *Students Speaking*, Teaching in Higher Education 6 (3) 2001, with Fiona Montgomery; *Questions of Gender*, in Brian Brivati and Richard Heffernan (eds.) Labour's First Century (MacMillan,2000); *The International Faith* in Berthold Unfried and Christine Schindler (eds.), Riten, Mythen und Symbole; Die Arbeiterbewegung zwischen 'Zivilreligion' und Volkskultur (Leipzig: Akademische Verlangsantalt, 1999); *Ernest Bevin and Edo Fimmen* in Bob Reinalda (ed.), The Fimmen Years (International Institute of Social History, 1997); *The Patience of a Saint and the Cunning of the*

Devil: Teaching Women's Studies in the 1990s, Teaching in Higher Education 1, (1) 1996, with Fiona Montgomery; *Daughter of the Newer Eve* in Jim Fyrth (ed.), Culture and Society in Labour Britain (Lawrence and Wishart,1995); *Gender and Class in the Labour and Socialist International* in Gabriella Hauch (ed.), Geschlecht, Klasse, Ethnizitat (Vienna,1993); *The Labour Party and the Labour and Socialist International*, Labour History Review, 58 (1) 1993; *So Utterly Forgotten: Irish Prisoners and the 1924 Labour Government*, North West Labour History 16, 1991/2; *Skandal bei den Sozialisten* in Logie Barrow et al (eds.), *Nichts als Unterdruckung? Geschlecht und Klasse in der englischen Sozialgeschichte* (Verlag Westfalisches Dampfboot,1991); *New Realism, Old Traditions: Reconciling Women's Experience*, Labour History Review, 56 (1) 1991; contribution to C.S. Nicholls (ed.), *Power: a Political History of the Twentieth Century* (Harraps,1990); *Socialism and Scandal*, History Workshop 23, 1987; *Socialist Feminism in Oxfordshire* Feminist Review 26, 1987; *An Independent Voice* North West Labour History 12,1987.

More from Circaidy Gregory Press

The Freak and the Idol
by Katy Jones

...for any woman who has ever watched a TV ad telling her she's worth it, and wondered why she's only worth a pot of moisturiser; and for any man who's ever been bemused by the length of time it takes a woman to put on her 'face'
– Catherine Edmunds
ISBN 978-1-906451-28-8
UK £8.99+P&P

red silk slippers
poems by Marilyn Francis

As surreal as a de Chirico creation perhaps, but this is an accessible, welcoming book of real-world poems – as real as those red silk slippers from Thailand.
ISBN 978-1-906451-13-4
UK £6.50 + P&P

Left of the Moon
by Monica Tracey

Family secrets and dramatic encounters reach from Ireland to Italy and across the generations.

'Monica Tracey writes with sympathy, warmth and wisdom' – Hilary Mantel

ISBN 978-1-906451-35-6
UK £7.49 + P&P

Down Bottle Alley
A play by Tom O'Brien

There's a 'Bottle Alley' in every town, but who are the people you find there, and what is a town to make of its vagrant alcoholics? As a Hastings town councillor put it, 'no-one leaves school with an ambition to become a street drinker.'
ISBN 978-1-906451-21-9
UK £7.99 + P&P

Available from your library, independent bookshop or buy online direct from...

www.circaidygregory.co.uk